American Harem

Krystal N. Craiker

Content Warnings

This book takes place in a future USA under a theocratic monarchy. Queerness is illegal in this world.

This book contains:

- Queerphobia

- Mentions of sexual assault and rape

- Mention of suicide

- BDSM/kink

- Cannabis use

- Mention of drug use and prostitution

- Death of family members

- Explicit scenes with multiple partners, all consensual

Also by Krystal N. Craiker

The Scholars of Elandria Fantasy Romance Series
The Sage's Consort
The Consort's Journey
The Sage's War

Historical Romance Standalone
Hell's Revenge: Memoir of a Pirate Queen

To Michael, who is far less broody but no less amazing than my
main character

1

The floor of the American queen's palace, where Miriam was to be executed, was pink. And not a bright, happy shade, either. More like black market antibiotics pink. Conversion camp dorm room pink.

Miriam hated pink.

She bit back the bile rising in her throat. This moment was inevitable. She had played with fire for too long, but that didn't ease her terror at all. Being ready to die for a cause was a lot different than actually dying.

She wished the cops had left the hood on to fight these waves of nausea. Guess she'd be meeting her demise surrounded by her own vomit.

No. Miriam blinked. Where was the courage that had guided her these last several years—hell, her whole life? She steeled herself and blinked in the harsh, fluorescent lighting. She would meet her fate with her head held high.

Her courage came back bit by bit as she raised her head. Now, if she could just keep from losing the contents of her stomach. Finally, she lifted her chin and used her bound hands to push her dark hair behind her ear.

Shock pushed away the bravery and the nausea. This didn't look like an execution chamber, or even a place for a hearing with Her Majesty. It looked like one of those fancy hotel rooms Miriam had seen advertisements for. A massive bed with a rose-printed duvet took up most of the room. Fine cherry-wood nightstands stood on either side, with a matching desk under a window on the opposite wall. A generic—and pink, of course—painting hung above the bed.

The armed security guard at the door wasn't like a hotel, though. A broad, dark-skinned man stood with a stoic expression, his arms crossed. He didn't look at Miriam but stared at the wall opposite him.

"Weird place to be executed," Miriam said just to see if he would move. He didn't so much as twitch. "Cool. Guess it's just you and me."

Miriam decided that whatever her fate, she might as well be comfortable. She stood on aching, bruised legs—those fucking cops were brutal—and dusted the grime off her black leather pants as best as she could. Of course, she couldn't have been caught in her pajamas or even her work clothes. Nope, leather pants and a corset. How fitting.

She sat cross-legged on the bed and waited for...what? She swallowed the beginning of a sob. No, she wouldn't cry in front of the guard. She didn't cry in front of anyone, and she wouldn't start now. She couldn't think about what came next. Whatever it was, she hoped it would be over quick. She'd heard the rumors about the torture that came when Queen Candace had demanded all Depraved be sent directly to the palace upon capture. The ruler of the Holy United States of America was a sick, twisted bitch.

There was no clock, so Miriam had no idea how long she sat. But eventually, she heard a beep from the door, which then slid open to reveal the queen bitch herself.

Oh, so this was personal. Would she do it herself or have her guard do it? Miriam raised her chin and narrowed her eyes. She wouldn't give respect to this woman, royal or not. Not when she kept queer people in the shadows; not when she killed them just for daring to be themselves.

Candace was shorter in person than she appeared on the screen. She had dyed blonde hair and an innocent face. In one hand, she held a Moses Tablet, which she scrolled through as she entered. When the door shut behind her, she looked up and smiled warmly at Miriam.

"Miriam Jefferson, we've looked for you for a long time. I assume you know why you're here...Lilith?"

Miriam said nothing. She waited. Of course she knew why she was here. Her persona, Lilith, was a dark web legend. And now her website, full of information about safety, sex, kink, and more, would never be updated again. She'd been a beacon in the darkness for the Depraved, and she was damn proud of it.

"Nothing to say? You have quite the list of capital sins."

Miriam took a deep breath. "I have nothing to be ashamed of. Are you just going to talk at me, or can we get this execution moving?"

Queen Candace flipped her blonde hair and turned back with a grin. "I'm just going to talk."

A strange feeling washed over Miriam. It wasn't fear, but anticipation. Something was off, and it didn't feel altogether evil. Maybe Candace was just that good at pretending.

Candace crossed the room and pulled out the desk chair. She perched, the very picture of dignity. Miriam didn't take her eyes off the queen. She didn't trust her as far as she could throw her.

"You're lovely," Candace said. "So much prettier than I imagined you'd be."

Talk about unexpected. "Uh, thanks?"

"From what we've gathered about you, I can tell you're a smart woman. An archivist, committing treason with high security clearance."

Miriam scoffed. "I guess a website is treason."

"Yours is." The queen shrugged. "It doesn't matter. You're smart. You know the world is dangerous for people like you."

"The world isn't. This country is."

Candace narrowed her eyes, just a bit, before putting a calm expression back on her face. Miriam almost questioned if her face had really changed. "Our world, then."

"And whose fault is that?" Miriam stood up. She couldn't hold her tongue. "You are why we live in secret."

Sadness flickered over Candace's face. "It's more complicated than that. The Supreme Court...well, it wouldn't be safe for you to be out. But that's what I'm trying to say." She gave Miriam a small smile. "I'm not going to kill you. I am trying to keep you—all of you—safe."

Miriam blinked. "You are the absolute ruler of the Holy USA."

"And if I suddenly declared that you weren't sinners, that you could come out, do you think everyone would agree? That you would all be safe?" She shook her head. She was right. There was far too much vileness and hatred in the country. "I'm here to offer you safety. A life where you're free to be yourself."

"What?" The room started spinning. Miriam sat down again. This was too much to take in.

"I'm bungling this." Candace took a deep breath. "Miriam,

you cannot go back to your old life. But I have two options for you. Well, one is more of a proposition."

Folding her arms across her chest, Miriam met Candace's eyes with a glare. "Go on."

"The first option is to work in one of my residences. It's taken years, but now all of my staff is queer, from my cleaners to my guards." Miriam's eyes stole over to the stoic guard. She could see it.

"And the second option?"

Candace smiled. "It's complicated. I have a group of people to attend to my needs. You could live there with no duty, save one."

Miriam's curiosity was piqued. She raised a brow. "And that is?"

"Lady Lilith, I need a Dominatrix."

Miriam burst out laughing. All the tension from her capture to now, hell, for the last decade, came out in roars of laughter. She struggled to catch her breath. "You're...you're joking."

"No, Miriam. I am not." The queen flipped her hair over her shoulder and stood. "I'm one of the Depraved."

Depraved. Miriam hated that word. There was nothing wrong with being queer. But that was the official term for them. "Is there a third option?"

The queen cocked her head to the side, thinking. "I could drop you at the DMZ, and you could try your luck in the desert."

The Demilitarized Zone, or DMZ, was a fifty-mile stretch of desert that was once part of Texas and the Southwest. As the Holy USA shrunk, Mexico agreed to a wide border lined by a massive, thousands-miles-long fence. The monarchy said it was to keep foreigners out, but no one was seeking refuge in the USA in 100 years.

"Can I think about it?" Miriam asked.

"Of course. Take a couple of days. Enjoy the room." The queen grinned at her. "I do hope you'll consider joining us." She waved over the stoic guard, who pulled a device that looked like a thick screwdriver from his pocket. "Apologies. We have to remove your chip. It will hurt, but we have nanobots to heal it quickly."

The guard took Miriam's hand, placed the device on the inside of her wrist where her identity chip had been since birth, and pressed a button.

"Son of a bitch!" The pain shot up her arm. The guard then placed a small bandage over the bleeding wound, and the pain subsided almost instantly. Miriam thought about how expensive nanotech was on the black market with disgust. It should be available to everyone—apparently it was in the rest of the world.

"Congratulations, Miriam," the queen said. "You officially no longer exist."

2

Asher pressed the button on the MolecuMaker, then leaned against the wall with his eyes closed as the sound of liquid generating into a cup echoed through the empty kitchen. He was exhausted. Sleep had eluded him last night. That was to be expected. He didn't anticipate sleeping much over the next few days. He never did this time of year.

"Generated whiskey? Why the fuck would you drink that?" a voice pulled him from his thoughts.

"Gets the job done." Asher opened eyes to find Elijah sniffing the cup inside the MolecuMaker. He couldn't help the small smile that loosened his lips at Daniel's crinkled nose. They'd been friends—and sometimes more—their whole lives, and Elijah was the only one who could crack Asher's foul moods. Not shatter them. No one could do that. But he could spare a smile for his friend today.

Elijah glanced up at the screen on the wall to see the date. "Oh, Ash. It's today. I'm sorry."

Asher shrugged one shoulder, dropping it slowly, any hint of good humor slipping away. He grabbed the cup of whiskey and took a swig. It was vile. Whoever had put the blueprint for whiskey in had selected whatever was below the bottom-shelf. But he'd be drunk and numb soon, as he planned to be for the next three days. But not the fourth. Never the fourth.

Elijah reached a strong, copper-brown hand out and squeezed Asher's upper arm. "It will be eight years on Friday?"

"Yeah."

His friend smiled. "Go. Keep your vigil. I'll track down something that tastes better."

Asher wasn't sure he deserved something that tasted better. "In another hour, it won't matter what it tastes like."

"She can spare something expensive. It's the least she can do." Elijah ran a hand through his dark, close-cut beard. "You know, if you want, I can join you. We don't have to talk. But if you want company…"

"Thanks, but I just want to be alone." He needed to be alone. Elijah meant well, but he never understood Asher's need for solitude.

Elijah straightened and planted a soft, familial kiss on Asher's cheek. "Drink some water, too."

Then he left. Asher was alone again. He downed the rest of the swill, replaced the glass inside the appliance, then pressed the button for more. For a moment, he thought maybe he'd change it up with a glass of rum or tequila, but thought better of it. Even Asher didn't hate himself enough to drink generated tequila.

He was properly drunk and full of extra self-loathing by the time Candace summoned him later that afternoon. "Fuck," he slurred to himself. She knew better. She knew to leave him alone while he grieved his sister. Something had to be wrong.

He rubbed his temples as he made his way to the elevator that led directly to Candace's penthouse apartment. He was not in any mood—nor any shape—to be advising her on anything today. He didn't think she had a meeting with the Supreme

Court for a couple of days. He couldn't remember in his drunken fog, though.

"What do you want?" he said as soon as the elevator doors dinged open. Candace sat on her overstuffed pink sofa, Moses Tablet in hand.

She glanced up and wrinkled her nose. "I can smell you from here. How much have you had to drink?"

"Not enough."

She heaved a sigh. "I know what today is, Asher. I'm sorry. This couldn't wait."

He stumbled toward a chair and sprawled out. "What happened?"

"We found her. Lilith."

Asher took a deep breath. Candace's fascination with the mysterious dark web persona bordered on infatuation. Personally, Asher thought they should have left her alone. Her website served an important function for the Depraved living in the shadows. But Candace had been trying to find her for years. Lilith, whoever she was, was elusive and smart.

"Is she here?" He rubbed his temples again. The headache was starting. Maybe he had had enough to drink.

Candace leaned forward with bright eyes. "Her name is Miriam. She's exactly how I imagined her. But somehow even more gorgeous."

"Candace..." Asher knew where this was going.

"I gave her a choice, Asher. I'm not going to force her into anything."

She'd already forced the poor woman into an impossible choice and ripped her away from her life. But this was the best way they knew to keep the queer community safe for now. If they didn't remove them from their lives, they'd end up dead once their secrets were out.

"And what was that choice?"

"The usual." Asher arched an eyebrow, and Candace huffed. "I need a Dominant, Ash. There's this side of me that needs it, yearns for it."

"You've got nine other people to sleep with, Candy."

"None of them are right. They're not—"

Asher held up a hand. "I get it. But do you really think this is the right person to fulfill those desires? She's been committing treason for years. She can't have any warm feelings toward you."

Candace shrugged. "It feels right. Besides, she hasn't given me an answer yet. I'm giving her a few days to decompress like I usually do."

"Candy, this is a bad idea. The relationship between a Domme and a sub is..." He waved a hand. "There's a power dynamic."

"I know, Asher. that's the whole point."

"You're the queen. You have too many enemies. Letting someone in who—"

Candace cut him off. "It's just about sex, Ash. Some scenes. I'm not going to let her control my life."

There was no convincing her. Once Candace was this set on something, even he couldn't change her mind. He rose and wandered over to the bar in the corner, grabbed a nice bottle of tequila, and said, "I hope you know what you're doing."

3

Fresh out of Candace's wardrobe MolecuMaker, and wearing tight, vintage-style denim and a bamboo and lace top, Miriam approached the locked double-doors to the harem. Because that's what it was. In the greatest fleece in history, the queen of the Holy USA had a bisexual harem of lovers hidden in her palace. Miriam's mind was still reeling.

She had taken Candace's proposition. How could she not? Scrubbing the floors of a vacation palace for the rest of her life wasn't appealing, even if she could be out as pansexual. A Domme/sub relationship was built on trust, which Miriam didn't have. But Candace had given her an opportunity. She didn't know how, yet, but perhaps she could wield some sort of power over the queen. Make a difference.

Until then, if she could just do nothing, with no constant stress of looking over her shoulder, she'd take it. Her entire life was ripped away from her. She'd never see her family again, not that they were close. She'd never frequent the dungeon or underground clubs again. Her existence was still a secret, but she was safe for the first time in her life.

"They're expecting you," Candace said. "I'll see you soon."

Miriam glanced up at the queen. She still hadn't curtsied or given any sign of respect, but Candace didn't seem to mind.

"You're not coming?"

She shook her blonde head. "We have an agreement. I only enter the Residence by invitation."

Brows raised, Miriam said, "Cool. And one week until we meet?"

"Yes, get settled in. But if you need anything, you can take that elevator"—she pointed down the hallway—"straight to my apartments."

Swallowing, Miriam straightened her shoulders. "Right. I guess this is it. My fate."

Candace gave her a warm smile. "Enjoy." She turned, her heels click-clacking on the pink marble floors, leaving Miriam alone.

Miriam cleared her throat. "Right. Here goes nothing." She stepped up to the entrance, where a retinal scanner beeped as it captured her eyes.

The double doors slid open to reveal a massive lounge full of plush furniture and Turkish style decor in rich, jewel tones. Candace had really taken the harem-style to heart. It was downright cliché, Miriam thought as she stepped in, with ornate rugs and vibrant tapestries warming the room. The lighting was warm, and there were no windows to brighten the room.

Two men, one blond and model-esque, the other with warm brown skin and a friendly smile, glanced up from a low sofa and waved at her. She gave a tiny wave back.

"Hi," she said.

"Hey," the Black man said, "I'm Isaac. This is Abel."

"What's up?" Abel said, then turned his head to holler, "She's here!"

Moments later, footsteps bounded down the staircase to Miriam's left. A slight, brown-skinned woman with silky black hair greeted Miriam with a grin. A huge, familiar grin.

"Sherah?"

"Miriam? Oh my God. Miriam! When she said your name was Miriam, I didn't think—"

Isaac laughed. "You two know each other?"

Sherah threw her arms around Miriam. "Yes! Conversion camp buddies."

"Oh, my God, it's been what? Fifteen years?" Miriam blinked away the tears that threatened to fall. "You dropped off social media a couple years ago, and I was so scared that—"

"I was caught leaving a club." Sherah didn't try to hide her tears. "But Candace took a liking to me and, well, here I am."

Sherah hugged Miriam tighter, then stepped back, wiping her tears. "You look fabulous." She placed a steadying hand across her stomach. "I can't believe it. I volunteered to show you around, and it's you."

It was all surreal. Miriam's heart pounded as her head tried to make sense of everything. "Do you think the queen knew?"

Isaac laughed again. "She's not that detail-oriented. I think you two just have a happy coincidence."

Miriam wasn't sure happy was the right word for any of this, but she was so glad to see a familiar face, even if they hadn't seen each other in years. They barely knew each other, but the things they had gone through at conversion camp, well, those memories bound them.

"Come on, let me show you around. This is the living room. You already met Isaac and Abel." Sherah leaned in and whispered. "Abel is an asshole."

"Noted." She followed Sherah through the living room. "How many of us are there?"

"You make ten." They went through glass doors into an indoor pool area with a fabulous pool and hot tub. Sun shone through the glass windows and glinted off the water. "We hang out in here a lot. The saltwater pool is heated. Through there is a gym if that's your thing. It's not mine."

"This is not what I pictured when Candace talked about the Residence."

Sherah groaned. "I'm pretty sure she likes to think we're just all down here having orgies all the time. She's ridiculous."

"So you're not?" Miriam laughed.

"We hook up sometimes. Well, most of us." Sherah shrugged. "Occasionally having to sleep with Candace isn't all that satisfying."

In the kitchen, complete with a food MolecuMaker, Miriam met Esther, a curvy brunette, Jez, a person with amazing blue hair, and Elijah.

"No fucking way. You're the Elijah Porter." It had made the news when the famous Black actor had been arrested for Depravity.

"In the flesh." He extended a hand. "Nice to meet you."

"This is too surreal. I'm going to be living with Elijah Porter."

He flashed a grin. "You'll quickly learn I'm not all that exciting."

Sherah nodded in agreement. "He knits. That's his thing." Miriam blinked. "We all have a hobby or something. Or two. You go crazy if you don't pick something to keep you occupied."

What would Miriam do with endless free time? She didn't even know where to start. "I guess I can't keep up my Lady Lilith blog from in here, huh?"

"Wait." Elijah leaned forward. "You're Lady Lilith? Oh my god."

"Who's Lady Lilith?" Esther asked.

"A hero," Elijah answered. "Her site was untraceable. It had everything you needed to know about being queer in the Holy USA." He embraced Miriam, who stiffened at the suddenness of it. "You helped me understand myself so much. Thank you."

Miriam realized that Elijah was more starstruck than she was. "You're welcome. I am glad I helped."

Elijah accompanied Sherah as she showed her around the rest of the residence. There were some random recreational rooms, bedroom pods that were just big enough for giant beds with dressers built into the walls, and, to Miriam's delight, a library with actual physical books.

And in the library was a tall man with glasses, reading a book in an armchair. He set the book down when they entered.

"Asher," Elijah said, "this is Miriam. She's Lady Lilith."

"I know." He stood, revealing just how tall he was. And how toned. Jesus Christ. Miriam always had a thing for the nerdy types, and his long lashes accentuated his honey brown eyes. He had perfect brown hair. "Hello, Miriam."

His voice was a tenor and smooth. And his handshake was strong, firm, and sent shivers down Miriam's spine.

"Hello. Nice to meet you."

He gave a half-smile and looked her up and down. "Welcome to Candace's collection."

They were still holding hands, Miriam noticed. She let go. "Collection?"

"It's what we are, isn't it? Some people collect tchotchkes.

Candace collects people."

"Pardon Asher," Elijah interjected. "He can be a bit of a downer." He gave Asher a look. "Dude."

"Sorry." He shrugged, not looking sorry in the least. "It's nice to meet you."

"Yeah," Miriam said. But he was right. Miriam was now nothing more than a trophy. Her entire purpose had been stripped from her. A dark cloud landed in her stomach. "Excuse me. Sherah, can you show me which room is mine?"

4

“All right boys, read 'em and weep.” Isaac laid out his cards to reveal a straight flush.

Groans sounded around the table, and chips clattered into the pit. Isaac was hard to beat. Asher was the only one who could consistently beat him, but that didn't stop guy's poker night from happening every Saturday. It helped to have some order and schedule in the Residence; otherwise, the days stretched, endless and meaningless.

But Asher wasn't doing well tonight. He was distracted, but thankfully, only Elijah seemed to notice. He noticed everything, but that didn't mean Asher would talk about it.

Daniel began shuffling the cards. “What'd y'all think of the new girl?” he asked in his high, Southern drawl.

“She's amazing,” Elijah said. “I can't believe we got the real Lady Lilith.”

“Eh. She's a little too chubby,” Abel replied. “Did you see the size of her—hey!” Isaac had thrown a piece of popcorn and nailed Abel in the head.

“What is wrong with you?” Asher shook his head. “You're such an ass.”

No one really liked Abel except Marah and Candace. And sometimes Isaac, who Asher suspected only liked Abel for his body. Abel had also put up a fight when Daniel came out and tried to say he couldn't be included in guy's night. Asher had put a quick stop to that mindset, and he had come around.

"You act like a straight man." Daniel made a perfect bridge with the deck of cards. "If we didn't all know how much you liked sucking dick..."

Abel folded his arms and pouted while everyone laughed. "So you all don't agree?"

"No!" A chorus of men's voices sounded.

Asher certainly didn't agree. Miriam was thick, yes, with curves a man could get lost in. Silky dark hair just begging to be pulled. She was a walking Sex Goddess, and that was dangerous. No one had tempted Asher in a long time, not since the Residence started certainly. He'd already guiltily rubbed one out in his room after Miriam left. And of course, her bedroom pod was across from his, so he could just imagine throwing open her door and...

Elijah nudged him. "Asher, your cards, man."

"Sorry." He picked up his hand and tried to make sense of them. "You know what? I'm out. I'm just not feeling well tonight." He tossed his cards down. "See you guys tomorrow."

He made his way to the library for some respite. A good, dry book would clear his mind. Something historical, maybe. Candace had collected quite the stock of banned books for Asher's library, and he made use of it often.

Shit. Miriam was here, standing in front of the fiction section. He took a moment to appreciate the view of her backside, all lush curves, then shook himself. He had to stop this.

Miriam glanced over her shoulder. "Oh, hey."

"Hey."

"I'm just looking for a book to keep me company. But I've never had so many options."

"I get it. Um, I can come back later if…"

She turned and smiled. "No, of course not. The library is plenty big enough for both of us."

She was right, and there was no graceful way to leave when all Asher wanted to do was run to his room. Instead, he grabbed a random book about Roman history off the shelves and sat in one of the leather armchairs. Then he tried not to look at her, but failed.

"I've only gotten to read three actual books in my life. Everything else was on the Moses Tablet." She was still studying the shelf, running her fingers along the spines.

"There's nothing quite like holding the words in your hand," Asher said.

Miriam smiled and glanced at him. "Almost like magic. If I believed in magic."

"Not a believer, then?"

She sneered. "I believe in myself. That's the only thing I can count on." She paused. "You?"

"I don't think I believe in anything." He smiled. "You're not alone in that thinking here."

"I've gathered. I think I've gotten just about everyone's life story in the past three days." She gave up on the shelf and plopped into the chair next to Asher, looking at him expectantly. "You've been here since the beginning, huh?"

"I've known Candace a long time." He was careful not to say too much, not to be too open.

"I was an archivist. Removed a lot of truth from our records to serve the story the country tells."

Asher nodded. "I know."

She cocked her head at him. "You seem to know a lot. And yet, no one seems to know much about you."

He smirked. "Asking about me then?"

"Maybe I just want to know about the people I have to spend the rest of my life with." But she blushed as she said it. "Here's what I've learned. You're surly."

"I won't deny that."

"You don't sleep with anyone except scheduled times with Candace."

He raised an eyebrow. He knew that's what everyone thought, but Asher didn't sleep with anybody.

"You're old friends with Elijah. And you seem to be kind of the leader around here."

He shrugged. "We don't have a leader. But I've been here the longest."

"That's it?"

Asher rubbed his eyes under his glasses. "That's it. I'm sure you'll learn more the longer you're here."

"No one else seems to have learned anything else."

"Everyone knows I can't turn down chocolate. And I'm allergic to kiwi."

She laughed. "Kiwi? See, that wasn't so hard. And who can turn down chocolate?"

"Marah. She hates sweets. And happiness." Marah and Abel were peas in a pod, always eager to start shit. Misery loved company, and it loved those two most of all. With only nine, now ten, residents, there was always an opportunity for drama in the harem.

"Good to know." She stretched and yawned. "Maybe I'll go watch some banned movie in my room instead. I'm overwhelmed by book choices."

"What do you like to read?" Asher asked. "I can recommend something. The choices...it's overwhelming when you have had none your whole life. It can drive you crazy."

Miriam sighed, which drew Asher's attention to her breasts as they rose and fell. Damn it. "I just want to escape."

"Don't we all?" He stood and headed to the fiction shelf, looking for a particular title. "Here. Dragons and magic. It's good."

She smiled up at him from beneath her lashes. "Thanks, Asher." She stood and left with the book in hand.

It was only then that Asher remembered he had also given her a book with two graphic sex scenes. What would she think about that? And now all he could think about was her reading those scenes.

Shit. He was in trouble.

5

"She's in a mood," Marah announced as she and Abel re-entered the harem, looking disheveled and freshly sexed.

Miriam glanced up from the tangle of blue yarn. In her attempt to find a new passion to occupy her time, Miriam had asked Elijah to teach her to knit. She was not very good at it, nor was she sure she cared to be. But she would finish this scarf, hideous though it may be.

"Why?" Esther piped up from the couch opposite Miriam. She was carving something out of wood with a knife. "What happened now?"

Abel shrugged. "Housing justice did something to piss her off."

Elijah spoke from next to Miriam without looking up from the perfect sweater he was knitting. "Didn't you watch the news? He tore down an entire neighborhood to build new mansions. And an education center. And shopping"

"So?" Abel asked.

"So," Elijah answered, "There's a whole neighborhood of people without homes who probably can't afford anywhere else."

"It puts a strain on the other departments like Agriculture

and causes discontent with the government," Esther added. "Do you have any critical thinking skills, Abel?"

Abel shook his head. "I'm too pretty for those." Marah slapped Abel on the back of the head.

Both Candace and the Supreme Court ran the Holy USA. Each Supreme Court justice controlled a pillar of the country. They owned every business within that pillar. Each had a privatized military, and several owned a news outlet. The news only ever reported in favor of what a justice did, but it was easy to read between the lines. There was discord happening among the crown and the court, though no one knew the details.

No one, it seemed, except some of the harem residents.

"So Candace and Justice Grant don't get along?" Miriam asked.

Everyone laughed. "Hell no," said Daniel, who had just entered with a bowl of cereal. He plopped down next to Esther. "Neither do Healthcare, Transportation, or Education. They actively work against whatever initiative Candace wants to do."

Miriam took this knowledge down. As an archivist, she knew that all information could be useful. "What about the others?"

Elijah spoke up this time. "Defense stays pretty neutral. Energy is more concerned with making more money than infighting."

"The Agriculture Justice is like a second father to Candace. He's loyal. And Candace gives a shit ton of money to Technology, so they do whatever she wants," Esther added.

A loud ding sounded that Miriam recognized as Candace's summoning. She glanced up at the large screen on the wall. The queen wanted Asher.

"Didn't she just get laid?" Isaac said.

"The fucking pillow princess sure did," Marah said. "We did all the work."

"I think you mean pillow queen," Abel said.

Footsteps bounded down the stairs, and Miriam looked up to see Asher dressed in a loose t-shirt and bamboo fabric shorts that highlighted an enticing bulge. Asher caught her eye as she stared and smirked at her.

Marah warned him that Candace was in a mood. "I know," he replied. "I saw the news."

He'd known Candace a long time, and they must be close if he could anticipate her moods. Miriam wondered, not for the first time, if they were in love. But if so, why have a harem full of lovers? She watched, admiring, as his firm back disappeared behind the residence doors.

6

Candace was still naked in her bed when Asher entered her luxe apartments. Asher sighed. "Can you put some clothes on when you summon me?"

"It's nothing you haven't seen before." She wriggled in what Asher assumed was supposed to be a sexy movement.

He looked up at the gilded ceiling. "That was a long time ago, Candace."

"And how you've changed."

He heard the bedding ruffle and creak as Candace moved. A moment later she said, "I'm decent."

Asher looked at her. He didn't consider the short, silk robe decent, but then again, it was her room. It wasn't that she was bad to look at. Candace was undeniably a beautiful woman. But he didn't view her in that way anymore. It was like looking at a cousin, and it made him feel uncomfortable. Then again, Asher didn't particularly desire or seek out anyone's naked body any more. Miriam flashed in his mind, and he cleared his throat.

"Housing?"

Candace suddenly looked years younger, her eyes round. "There was so much yelling. Noah Westcott was angry. Reminded me of Dad."

Asher crossed over and gave her a hug, then sat on the leather bench at the end of the massive bed. "And did you do any yelling?"

Her shoulders slumped. "I just get all tongue-tied."

"Candy," Asher said, "you've got to start earning their respect. For the country."

"I'm not cut out for this." She shook her head. "They think I'm weak."

Asher shrugged. "You're acting weak."

"That's not making me feel better."

"If you want someone to make you feel better, get one of the others, Candy." He leaned back on the bench and stretched out his tall frame. "You want me to be your advisor, then let me advise."

"It's just—"

"People are suffering, Candy. You have to play the game with the justices. You have to keep them loyal to you."

"How?"

"Don't give them a reason to walk all over you. Kiss their old, hairy asses and win them over." She'd been trying for years, but they usually made her cower.

"They'll never respect me, Asher."

He removed his glasses and rubbed them on his shirt, thinking. "You can still help with the latest situation. What are you going to do about it?"

She blew air harshly out of pursed lips. "Food is already being sent."

There wasn't much else she could do. The crown didn't own any buildings near the displaced neighborhood, and Healthcare would offer no help.

"Can you write a statement for Jonathan?" Candace asked.

The Prime Minister for God couldn't write his own speeches for shit because he was usually high off his ass, but he stayed loyal to Candace. Asher had often written something for him to say on the national news.

"Some sort of prayer for the unhoused?"

"Yeah, that will work."

Advising Candace was a balancing act. Too many of the justices hated her because she was a woman or young or they didn't like her father. Or maybe they were just power-crazed. But if she pushed too hard, exerted too much power, people could die. Every justice had a military force, and there were still too many zealots living in the Holy USA. Mostly the rich and privileged—everyone else was too busy trying to survive.

Candace plopped down on the bed and propped her head up with her hand. "Let's change the subject. What do you think of Miriam?"

A grin spread over Asher's face before he could school his expression. Candace's eyes widened. Damn it, she knew him too well. "Miriam's nice."

The queen leaned forward. "She's pretty, don't you think?"

"Mm. Sure." He tried to sound noncommittal because he couldn't outright lie. Miriam was gorgeous.

"You think she's hot, don't you?"

Asher rubbed his eyes under his glasses. "I'm still human, Candy. I can appreciate her aesthetic."

"You know, a little sex wouldn't hurt you."

He rolled his eyes. "I'm not interested," he lied. "Besides, she's here to be your plaything."

"I'm supposed to be her plaything." She sat up, excited. "Tomorrow is a week. I get to spend time with her. Has she settled in okay?"

Asher thought about Miriam crying alone in the hot tub the night before. He had slipped away before she saw him. "As well as could be expected. Her whole life was stripped away."

"I know. But she has everything she needs now. She can live freely."

Asher wasn't in the mood to argue. Candace believed life in the harem was all sunshine and sex, when in reality, it was a luxury prison. But the alternative—the history—was so much worse. If people believed that all the Depraved were being dealt with by the crown, then they wouldn't take matters into their own hands. Violence had stayed sky high after the Second Great Ablution thirty years before, but vigilante justice had dropped to nearly zero after Candace started her initiative to save all the queer people.

They might lose everything else, but at least they didn't lose their lives anymore.

"Be careful, Candace. You know how intense a Domme/sub relationship can be..."

"Oh, I remember." She wiggled her eyebrows. Asher glared at her. "Sorry."

"She has a lot of reasons to hate you. Do you think you need someone else? A guard?"

Candace laughed. "Are you volunteering?"

Asher inhaled at the image that flashed in his mind—Miriam in leather, whip in hand, standing over Candace. Or someone. It didn't matter who. He shook himself mentally.

"I'm serious, Candy. Do you think she trusts you? How can you be her submissive if you don't have mutual trust?"

"She's not going to kill me, Asher." Candace laughed. "Don't be ridiculous."

7

It would be entirely too easy to kill the queen right now, Miriam thought as she passed a sheet of paper across the desk to Candace. She had handwritten a yes-no-maybe sheet with every kink she could think of. She wondered if the list would scare her, but then again, the woman did have a queer harem downstairs.

But Candace read eagerly, marking things off. They were alone in the queen's apartment. Miriam had never killed anyone, but she was strong. And she knew how to cut off someone's air supply. Usually they were willing, though.

But it would be obvious who killed the bitch of a queen, and Miriam had already escaped death. She wasn't sure she wanted to press her luck. And, to be honest with herself, she wasn't sure she was capable of murder, even if the queen was the ultimate evil. So she put her homicidal fantasies aside and watched as Candace completed the checklist.

It was a long list, and Candace was clearly putting great thought into it, which left Miriam plenty of time to think. And she had a lot to ponder about the last few days. Candace had made her feel like nothing short of an honored guest before she entered the harem. She'd left Miriam alone, but Miriam enjoyed a giant, luxurious bathtub and plush bed. She'd eaten the best she'd ever eaten in her life--three meals a day, cooked by a chef, with whatever snacks she could request. She'd also gained access to the queen's wardrobe MolecuMaker and built an entirely new, custom wardrobe.

Then, after three days, Candace had taken her to the harem. And what an experience that had been. She was slowly getting to know everyone in the Residence, as they called it (when they didn't call it what it was). Jez was a nonbinary person who was already on their second hair color since Miriam had arrived. They had a great laugh and could often be found composing music. Esther was a gorgeous woman with luscious curves and an affinity for baking and carving. Daniel was a trans man who kept to himself a lot, but was friendly enough. She hadn't figured out what he did besides hanging out in the pool. Marah and Abel were the gossips. They knew everything about everyone in the palace and had plenty of opinions on the matter. Marah was apparently quite skilled at chess, but Miriam didn't care to learn the game. Isaac was sweet and a talented painter.

Elijah and Sherah had already decided they would be Miriam's best friends in the Residence. Elijah was knitting Miriam a blanket because "everyone needed some item of comfort here." Sherah wrote poetry and short stories, but Miriam hadn't asked to read any yet. Miriam didn't know how to have close friends. It never paid to get attached to someone who could be arrested or killed at any moment. She wondered how many of her former acquaintances were working in the palace and which had just ended up dead in a ditch. It was a sobering thought, but a realistic one. If someone didn't take out the Depraved, they often fell victim to their own demons.

And then there was Asher. God, he was fucking gorgeous

and smart. Cynical. He was friendly enough, but he also seemed to dislike Miriam at times. She couldn't figure out why, except maybe he was jealous. From what she'd learned, the only person he slept with was Candace. Maybe he was in love with the queen, and if that was the case, Miriam should stay far away from him. Anyone who could love a monster like that couldn't be trusted.

But then she'd caught him staring at her more than once from across the room. And she wasn't afraid to admit to herself that she had admired him from a distance more than once. He was reserved, but he smiled and joked around with the others some. She just couldn't get a good read on him. It had only been a few days, though. Surely she'd figure him out soon enough.

"Finished!" Candace chirped.

Miriam sighed and took the papers, trying and failing to care about what it said. "Any questions?"

"Should I go ahead and get undressed or...?"

"Whoa. What?" Miriam shook her head. "We're not playing today, Your Majesty. I haven't even had time to review this."

Candace puffed out her lower lip. "But—"

"But nothing." How far could she go with setting boundaries with the queen? This was a serious one, though. "It wouldn't be safe. What if I did something you were a no on because I haven't had time to memorize this?"

Candace shrugged. "There are very few nos."

Miriam closed her eyes and took a deep breath. "No. I don't want to hurt you--physically or otherwise." That was a lie, but, Miriam found, not as much of a lie as she expected. It was hard to remember that Candace was the same person responsible for so much of the evil and suffering in the country.

"Please," Candace begged, reminding Miriam of a sullen teenager. It was, unfortunately, hard to resist. "I haven't been able to stop thinking about this. About you." She batted her eyelashes.

"So, you want sex, too."

Candace's eyes widened. "Of course! Why wouldn't I?"

"Because not all Domme/sub relationships are—you know what? Never mind." She huffed out a loud sigh. "We're not doing anything serious today, but you need to show me you know how to be a proper submissive."

Instantly, Candace dropped to her knees. She placed her hands in her lap and dropped her head to look at the floor. Miriam gaped in shock. Clearly, someone had taught Candace before. But who? And where were they now? She looked so comfortable in this position. Vulnerable.

That peaceful feeling Miriam got whenever she slipped into her role as a Domme warmed her from her toes to her cheeks. She rolled her neck, loosening all the tension of the past few days. It would be a long time before she lost the tension of a lifetime in the shadows, but maybe this was a start. Maybe they could have a mutually beneficial situation here. And Miriam could somehow, some day, make Candace pay for her sins.

"Crawl to the bed," Miriam ordered, her voice low.

Candace crawled without hesitation, her pert ass bobbing in the air. A giddy sense of power washed over Miriam. She had the queen crawling across the pink carpeted floor.

"Take off your clothes."

Candace started to unbutton her polka-dot blouse, but Miriam cleared her throat. "No. You need to answer me. You can address me as Mistress."

"Yes, Mistress."

Interesting. Miriam would have had Candace pegged as a brat, but it seemed she was eager to comply. To be forced into action. Later, she could puzzle over the psychology of it. But for now, she just wanted to feel her power.

She watched as Candace undressed. She wasn't unattractive by any means, with a slim figure and round breasts. Her pubic hair was dark and waxed into a line. Miriam's mouth watered against her will.

"Kneel."

"Yes, Mistress."

The queen knelt. Her gaze rose up to look at Miriam expectantly, but she kept her head bowed. Miriam made her sit there nude for several long minutes before she spoke again.

"That will be all for today. I'll be back in three days once I've had time to review your list."

Candace inhaled sharply and dropped her gaze. Her cheeks were red. But she nodded.

"I can't hear you," Miriam said.

"Yes, Mistress."

8

Miriam moaned and gazed down her body. Beneath her round, soft belly, she could just see the top of Sherah's head. "Fuck, that feels amazing, Sherah. Don't stop."

Sherah responded by swirling her tongue around Miriam's clit. Miriam closed her eyes and relaxed into Sherah's pillow. She ran her hands over her breasts and tweaked her nipples, and Sherah continued to strum and play between her legs. It had only been a week since Miriam had entered the Residence. Ever since the beginning of a scene with Candace, she'd been hornier than she could deal with. She had casually mentioned this to Sherah and Elijah earlier that day, and Sherah had given her a wicked grin.

"I could help with that," Sherah had said.

"Oh?" Miriam had responded. "I hadn't been implying, but..."

"Can I watch?" Elijah had asked.

One thing had led to another, which is how Miriam now found herself getting amazing head from an old friend while her new friend stood in the corner, somehow ignoring the erection straining his pants. "Jesus, you are good at that," Miriam gasped. She'd already come once thanks to Sherah's tongue and fingers and was getting close to coming again.

Sherah removed her head. "If you're able to get out sentences, I'm not doing my job well enough."

Miriam wanted to disagree, but then Sherah slid three fingers inside her, and Miriam bucked her hips off the bed. "FUU—"

"That's better," Sherah murmured against Miriam's vulva. Then, she set to work making Miriam come again, and hard.

"You're fucking gorgeous, you know that?" Elijah asked. "When you come, you look like an angel."

Miriam panted and propped herself up on her elbows. "So you're a voyeur, huh?"

Elijah looked down at the floor. Miriam quirked an eyebrow. "There's nothing wrong with your kink."

"I know." He shuffled a bare, brown foot against the rug lining Sherah's tiny bedroom. Sherah stood and began to dress, to Miriam's dismay. She had perfect, perky little breasts that deserved to be uncovered all the time.

Miriam turned her attention back to Elijah. He'd still made no move to address his hardness. Hadn't asked for help or anything. "Unless there's some other kink that you're feeling some shame about..."

Elijah's head snapped up. "You're good."

"It's my job. Or it was. Well, my night job, I guess." She shook her head. "No matter. Look, if you want to talk about anything that's in my wheelhouse of expertise."

Elijah looked at Sherah and sighed. "Maybe later."

"You can't tell me?" Sherah asked. "But Elijah..."

"Sometimes it's easier to discuss these things with a new person. Or a Domme," Miriam offered. "I wouldn't take it personally, Sher."

Sherah gave Elijah a hug. "I'm always here for you. No

judgment."

He wrapped his arms around her, and Miriam smiled as she sat up and began to pull on her tank top. She had decided that bras were an unnecessary form of torture, now that she lived with and saw only nine other people every day. Ten if she counted Candace.

"Come on, Elijah, let's go find a spot to talk." Miriam shimmied on her underwear and pants. She planted a quick kiss on Sherah's cheek. "Thanks, doll."

"I've been wanting to do that since we were seventeen," Sherah said.

Miriam winked. "Same. Maybe I can return the favor later."

They opened the door into the hallway at the same time that the door next to them opened. Asher sucked in a deep breath as he stared at Miriam and Elijah. His gaze swept over Miriam from the top of her head down to her feet.

"Hey, Ash," Elijah said. Miriam just smiled. Had he heard them? The thought made her heart pound, and she didn't know why. Asher had mostly avoided her, except when she caught him staring at her. But he was gorgeous and broody and smart, and something about him intrigued her.

Asher cleared his throat. He hadn't said anything for several moments. "Hey. Uh. Having fun, I guess?" He blushed.

So he had heard them, or at least heard Miriam. She wasn't exactly quiet when she came. But he lived here to fuck the queen, and it was clear that sex was pretty common in the Residence. Interesting that he didn't partake, but surely he was past blushing about it.

"A blast," Miriam said in a sultry voice. "Sorry if I disturbed you." She realized she didn't sound sorry at all.

"You didn't," he said in a strained voice.

"Well, good." She shifted her weight from foot to foot. This was awkward, and she wasn't sure why. "Well, we were just--"

"Yeah, I've got to go."

Miriam wasn't sure where he had to go. The Residence was already feeling a little small. With a shake of his head, Asher walked past Elijah and Miriam in the direction of the library.

Miriam stared after him. "That was weird."

"Asher's complicated," Elijah replied, but he was also staring after his friend. "He's my best friend, but he's a tough nut to crack."

Miriam turned to him and smiled. "Speaking of tough nuts to crack, let's see if I can help you out. My room?"

Miriam's room was right across from Asher's. She slid open the door and let Elijah enter first. Sherah's room had all sorts of personal touches and decor, but Miriam's was still sterile, with a generic white comforter on the bed and no rug or decorations on the walls. She sat on the edge of the bed and patted the spot next to her.

Elijah sat. It took him several minutes before he spoke, and Miriam didn't push him. Finally, he said, "I sometimes have trouble coming."

Miriam nodded. "Okay. When?"

He took a deep breath. "Most of the time with other people."

"Most? So when can you come?"

He squeezed each of his left fingertips with his right hand, a nervous tic Miriam had noticed. She patted his knee. "It's okay, Elijah. I've heard just about everything."

"How?"

She shrugged. "At the clubs, mostly. People often sought us

out just so they could talk about their desires and issues."

"You're easy to talk to."

She smiled. "Thanks."

"I can only come in one position. From behind."

"Top or bottom?"

"Either." He took a steadying breath. "If anyone is looking at me, I get...anxious. But I also don't like..." He trailed off.

Miriam curled her legs underneath her to get more comfortable. "I think you're a sub, Elijah."

"Yeah. I think so. From what I've read on your website, anyway. But I don't know." He shook his head. "It makes me feel like such a freak. I've always been this way."

It was interesting, Miriam thought to herself, that a man who had lived in the limelight as an actor for so long couldn't bear to be looked at during sex. Or maybe that was why. Kink was like that sometimes. Sometimes there was a deeper reason for what a person wanted and needed in their most intimate moments, but sometimes it just was who they were.

"That's okay, you know."

"I've learned to sort of fake it. At least with Candace—she can't tell whether I come or not."

Candace was clearly not a very attentive sexual partner. Miriam had heard other things that suggested that. Or maybe the bitch just didn't care one way or the other. Miriam refrained from rolling her eyes in case Elijah thought it was directed at him. She thought for a moment.

"Have you ever tried a mask?"

Elijah looked up, surprised. "Like a gimp mask?"

"Yes, or even just something over your eyes."

"Damn, you're really good." He rubbed a hand over his face.

"I haven't, but I often think about it. I think I've read the gimp post on your site a dozen times. I just worry about what people will say."

Miriam sighed. "You know, for a literal harem, there are some serious hang-ups about sex in this place." She'd just heard Abel complaining about eating out earlier that day. And Marah had alluded that some of the kitchen staff were into some "weird stuff."

"I wouldn't even know where to get one."

Miriam raised an eyebrow. "Surely someone here knows how to hack a MolecuMaker."

"Do you?"

She grinned. "Well enough. I'm just not good at designing inputs."

"I'm sure Isaac could help. He's a great designer."

Miriam leapt up. "This place needs some toys. Let's go find Isaac. We'll need to use one of the bigger MolecuMakers."

"Will Candace let us?"

"Candace is one kinky bitch." Miriam folded her arms. "I'm sure if she sees how it will benefit her, she'll be more than happy to let us design some sex toys." She gave Elijah a wink. "Besides, I can always order her to."

9

The library was dark, save for one lamp for Asher to read by. He preferred it this way at night. No one would assume he was in the library, up for a chat. He'd always had trouble sleeping, and it had been worse since his sister had died. At least he was safe here, and the library felt the safest of all.

He was trying to concentrate on a book about the history of flight and the Orville brothers. It had been holding his interest until today. Until he'd heard Miriam come in the room across from him. And oh, how beautiful she moaned. He'd been half-hard all day and had taken a cold shower that evening.

He wanted her. He wanted her so badly, but he couldn't have her. Not without dishonoring his sister's memory. He was screwed. He'd tried to keep his distance from her, but it was hard in the Residence.

Footsteps sounded in the hall. Probably someone creeping from someone else's bed to their own or headed back from a session with Candace. He wasn't sure what Miriam had done to her, but the queen had been insatiable for the last two days.

"Oh, fuck. S-sorry."

Asher glanced up at Miriam's voice. Fuck. Of course it was her. She was wearing a tank top and linen shorts, and she looked delectable.

She was also shaking.

"Miriam? Are you okay?"

She nodded, then shook her head no. "I d-don't..." She pressed her hands against her eyes. "I'm a mess."

The novelty of safety wore off after a few days. Then reality set in. They were stuck in another sort of prison, with no contact to the outside world. He didn't even know if she had loved ones she left behind. A partner, perhaps. He ignored the twinge he felt at that thought and stood.

"You're not a mess."

She let out a half-sob. "I don't cry."

"I won't tell anyone if you do." He crossed the few steps toward her. "So, your new reality set in?"

Now that he stood closer, he could see the tears streaming down her cheeks. She was still shaking, too. So, he did the only thing that felt right—he closed the distance between them and folded her into his arms. She stiffened at first, then her muscles relaxed and she sagged against him. Her sobs filled the air as she cried into his chest.

"I-I just keep"—she hiccuped—"I keep thinking about my parents."

"Were you close?" he asked in a low voice. He breathed in the strawberry scent of her shampoo.

She shook her head against his chest. "I don't even know if they know yet. And when they figure it out..." She whimpered and trembled.

"I know," he said. "I know."

He didn't, really. His situation was different. But he'd seen enough people come and go in the Residence that he understood this grief. And it wasn't like Asher was a stranger to the kind of grief that threatened to swallow one whole. Grief filled with shame and regret. Full of what ifs and whys. No, Asher lived that every single day of his life.

"And all the people I've let down. The site, the club…"

"Shhh. It will all be all right." He immediately regretted his choice in words and backtracked. "It's not all right. But it's okay that you're feeling this way."

She lifted a hand to wipe her eyes. "Why are you being so nice to me?"

Asher's eyes widened in response, but she wasn't looking at his face. "What do you mean?"

"Nothing," she said. "Forget it."

He inhaled. "I'm sorry I haven't been too friendly to you."

"It's fine." She stepped out of his embrace and gave him a sorry attempt at a watery smile. "I know you and Candace are—"

"Candace and I have known each other for a long time. But it's no excuse for me being an ass." He cleared his throat. "It's not you. It's just, this week is…well. It's no excuse."

"Sorry to bother you."

He waved a hand. "You're not bothering me." An idea struck him. "Come with me. I know what will help."

She shrugged. "Okay."

He led her down the hallway toward his room. "Wait right here." Then he went inside and dug around in a drawer to find what he was looking for. He gave her a half-smile when he exited his room. "This way."

She followed him as he led her through the dark hallways and empty rooms of the Residence toward a back staircase. He opened the door and flipped a light switch, then gestured for her to climb ahead of him. A terrible idea, he realized instantly, because he got a perfect view of her ass as she climbed the stairs.

"Are you taking me somewhere to murder me?" she asked. It sounded like only half a joke, and he knew she still wasn't convinced of her safety here in the harem.

"Just trust me," he replied. They climbed three flights of stairs and reached a landing with one door and an old-style lock. No sensors or retinal scanners. "Here we are."

"Where are we?"

He didn't say anything as he unlocked the bolts and pushed the door open. It was dark outside, but a few stars were visible. The palace was far enough from the capital city to escape most of the smog. It was the closest to fresh air Miriam had ever been. Garden beds of flowers, herbs, and shrubberies lined a few paths on the rooftop terrace. A few solar lamps offered enough light to guide their steps. In the far distance, the very beginnings of a pale light tickled the night sky.

"A garden?" Her voice was a whisper full of wonder.

"A garden," he agreed. "Come on."

He led her slowly down the path toward an area where two chairs perched on the edge of the rooftop. This was the backside of the palace, and when the sun was up, mountains would stretch in front of them. He sat down in a chair and gestured for her to sit next to him. Then he rummaged in his pocket and pulled out the joint and lighter he'd gotten from his room.

She let out a loud cackle. "Oh my god, you're my hero."

He tried to ignore the way his heart swelled when she said that. Instead, he lit the end of the rolled paper and passed it to Miriam as she sat down.

He watched as she took a long drag, rolled her head from

shoulder to shoulder, then exhaled. She gave one small cough, then passed the joint to Asher.

He inhaled, letting calm wash over him as the smoke filled his lungs. They sat in silence as they passed the cannabis back and forth between them. The stars faded as slivers of light from the east filled the sky.

Miriam let out a giggle, a musical sound that Asher thought might be the most beautiful thing he'd ever heard. He glanced over at her. "What's funny?"

"Your face."

Asher let out a laugh. "Real mature."

"No!" She laughed harder. "Your face earlier. After Sherah and I—"

"Oh." He pictured what his face must have looked like. God, he'd been so flustered. He blanched. "Yeah."

"You seem pretty prudish for living in an actual harem." She paused, then guffawed. "Oh my god, we live in a harem."

Prudish? Asher was far from it. But he couldn't explain that he'd been flustered because he'd been picturing Miriam making that noise for him. Imagining she lay beneath him, his to do with what he pleased. First, that wasn't the type of person Miriam was. She was in control all the time. And second, well, telling her would border too close to flirting, and he couldn't open that door.

He took another long drag off the joint because he was not high enough yet. His thoughts calmed down to a slower trot rather than a race, and he thought about what she'd said. He snorted. Sometimes, the ridiculousness of living in an actual harem hit him. Candace and her fucking ideas. But the other thing, Miriam had said...he felt like he had to let her know.

"I'm not prudish," he said in a low voice.

"What?" She stopped giggling and looked over at him. The sky was getting light enough that he could almost make out the green in her hazel eyes. Her round cheeks were flushed, and her kissable lips were slightly parted.

Asher sighed. "I'm not a prude."

Miriam cocked an eyebrow at him. "Is that so?"

Without meaning to, he leaned forward toward her. "It is."

Her breath hitched, and she reached out a hand to gently stroke down the side of his face. He shivered. Her soft fingertips trailed down his shoulder, over his arm, to his hand. She drew a small circle on the back of his hand before plucking the joint from his fingertips. He watched as her breasts raised and lowered as she inhaled the cannabis, the skunky smell somehow arousing in this moment.

She was dangerous. He wanted her so badly.

They said nothing as the sky lightened into shades of gold and pink. She looked like one of the heavenly host, showered in bright swaths from the sunrise. He found he couldn't take his eyes off her. For her part, she mostly ignored his gaze, but every now and then, she smiled and her cheeks turned pink.

Eventually, they made their way back to the Residence. Outside of their rooms, they paused. For a moment, Asher thought Miriam would kiss him, and he thought he'd let her, though that would be a mistake. But she simply whispered her thanks and disappeared into her room.

In his own bed, Asher groaned into his pillow. If he believed in a god, he'd wonder if Miriam was sent her to test him. An angel in disguise. He thought of her in the lowlight of the rooftop terrace, his cock growing hard beneath him. He shoved his shorts down and furiously, quickly beat himself to climax.

Awash in shame, he cleaned himself up and lay back down with a yawn. Maybe he could get a few hours of sleep. He turned on his side, facing the empty side of his bed.

Asher was often alone, and he preferred it that way. But right now, he'd never felt so lonely in his life.

10

Miriam woke a few hours later, after sleeping the best she had in the two weeks since she arrived at the palace. She needed to ask Asher where he was getting the weed from because clearly she needed some help sleeping. It had been nice to unwind with a little plant help. Finding cannabis in the city hadn't been impossible, but she rarely wanted to spend her money on it. And they never allowed it in the clubs because it could dull reaction times and pain sensations, and that was never a safe idea with kink.

She stretched and groaned in her bed. Wow, she had really needed last night. And who would have thought Asher would be the one to come to her rescue. She hadn't meant to cry into his arms. Literally. She grimaced—showing weakness like that was never ideal. But he'd been so warm, so kind, and so sturdy in her tearful display.

And then there was that moment on the terrace. Her body heated just remembering how it felt to trail her fingers over his skin. She wanted him. Before last night, she had no problems admitting to herself that she found him attractive. And sure, his broody act was intriguing. But last night, she'd wanted him, and she still did this morning.

She pictured his tall frame and imagined how chiseled his

chest must look. It felt hard beneath her last night. She hadn't paid much attention, but he must spend time in the gym. Surely he did things that weren't reading in the library or playing poker with the guys. Her hand cupped a breast, then trailed over her stomach, but just as she was inching her way inside her shorts, the screen on her wall beeped.

Glancing up, she let out a stream of expletives. It was her calendar, the only way she was able to keep track of the days here. Her first scene with Candace started in an hour. The last thing she wanted to do was see the bitch. She pressed the heels of her hands to her eyes and groaned. She still didn't know how she was going to handle sex. She didn't want to include that in this relationship, situationship, whatever. And though she was supposed to be the Domme, Candace was the literal queen. Could she have Miriam removed from the Residence? Make her clean toilets instead? Or worse, maybe she'd have her executed like she was supposed to.

Miriam shivered and pushed that thought from her mind. She would figure it out later, she guessed. Stretching one last time, Miriam pulled herself upright and rummaged through the drawers in the wall. The room was so small she could reach it from her bed. She pulled out a pair of leather pants and a corset that she'd had the MolecuMaker form for her. Getting this outfit on would be the real test of the machine's ability to take measurements.

But they fit like a glove, better than any leather she'd ever owned before. She took a long look at herself in the full-sized mirror then combed her hair and swept it into a bun. She'd requested some makeup, and a package had been delivered the day before. She never wore much, but she lined her eyes with kohl-black eyeliner and put on some magnetic lashes. She added a bit of color to her cheeks and painted her lips crimson.

Ready as she'd ever be, Miriam gathered up Candace's checklist, slipped her lipstick in between her cleavage, and went downstairs to find some coffee.

In the kitchen, she found Abel and Marah talking shit about some housekeeper or another. They glanced up when Miriam entered the room.

"Whoa," Marah said. "You look hot."

Miriam smiled. "Thanks. So do you." And Marah was hot—her ivory skin and curves were accentuated by the blue sundress she was wearing.

"Not like you, though. Hot damn. Abel, doesn't she look hot?"

Abel gaped a little at her, then gave a jerky nod. "Scene with Candace today?"

"In about a half hour."

"It's all she can talk about," Marah said. "Wait till she sees you in Full Domme Mode."

Miriam winked. "That's the secret, Marah. I'm always in Full Domme Mode." She pressed the button on the MolecuMaker and leaned against the wall while her coffee with hazelnut creamer generated.

Asher entered the kitchen and froze when he saw her. His mouth dropped, and he just stood there in the doorway. Miriam smirked. "Good morning."

He visibly shook himself. "Morning."

"See? I told you that you looked good. Even Asher the monk sees it," Marah said. Asher flipped her off.

Miriam folded her arms across her chest, knowing full well

what it did to her breasts. "Hey, thanks for last night, Asher. I needed that."

Asher looked quickly at Marah and Abel, who looked intrigued, and said, "It was nothing. Sometimes you just need a little smoke on the roof."

Abel's shoulders slumped. He grabbed his mug and left, Marah hot on his heels.

"It was more than that, and you know it," Miriam said in a low voice. Asher drew his gaze up to her eyes, his own eyes wide. "Thank you for comforting me."

He exhaled. "It's a strange new world you're living in."

"Yeah. Hey, about this strange new world, how do I get my hands on some of that good green?"

"Jez. They grow it up on the roof. But I can show you how to get rolling papers from the generator later."

Miriam smiled and took a sip of her coffee. "I'd like that."

Asher's cheeks turned red, and Miriam knew he was just as into her as she was into him. Last night had been about more than comfort and a smoke. She wished she had gone ahead and kissed him before turning in for the night. Maybe she wouldn't have woken up alone. Of course, Marah called him Asher the monk, so perhaps it wouldn't have gone anywhere.

Asher grabbed a mug and gestured at the wall. "Can I get some coffee?"

"Oh, sure. Sorry." She bit her lip and moved to walk past him. He wore athletic shorts and a different t-shirt from last night. She brushed her hip against him as she walked by, then reached up to pat his chest. "Thanks again, Asher."

She heard him inhale as she left the kitchen. When she turned around, she caught him watching her ass. He blushed, and she smiled. "Have a good day."

Miriam finished her coffee and set the mug on a low table in the main room. She touched up her lipstick, then made her way to the private elevator that led to Candace's rooms. She hummed a little tune to herself and thought about Asher. At least she knew beyond any doubt now that he was attracted to her. Maybe no one else had ever taken Asher to bed besides Candace, but no one else was Lady Lilith.

Upstairs, she found Candace in a most unexpected position. She hunched over the rosewood table in the living room of her apartment, her head in her hands. She sniffled and wiped her eyes.

Shit. What was Miriam supposed to do about a crying queen?

"Uh...do you want me to come back later?"

Candace raised her head, noticing Miriam for the first time. "No. Stay, please."

Miriam took a deep breath. "Are you okay?"

Candace's smile wavered. "I'm trying to be."

"What's wrong?" God, Miriam hated herself for caring. But even she couldn't ignore someone crying, even if that person was a murderous despot.

"Pierce is an ass." Miriam racked her brain before she realized that Candace referenced Levi Pierce, the Supreme Court justice who also controlled the healthcare in the country. He had to be one of the most evil of all the evil men on the Court. Ass was an understatement. Miriam just stared, waiting for Candace to continue. "He's refusing to send any aid to those displaced by Grant and the Housing Force, even after I said I would pay."

Evil didn't begin to cut it.

"They're all in close quarters, and people are getting sick,"

Candace explained. "And then he told me I shouldn't worry my 'pretty little head' over the people."

Miriam plopped down on a sofa and folded her arms. "You're the queen. Why can't you do something?"

"I'm trying! I sent some of my military doctors, and Alderman, the justice over Defense, agreed to send some resources. But the court moves against me at every step. Healthcare is a business, and I have no control over that."

Capitalist theocracy was what the rest of the world referred to the Holy United States as. Reuben Alderman was the nephew of the previous justice who ran the Defense division, and he had mostly stayed off the screens and out of the news. Sounded to Miriam like maybe he was less evil than the rest of them. Candace had her own military, as did every one of the eight industries controlled by the justices. But Defense had the largest and most well-equipped, as they maintained the borders.

A vein throbbed in Miriam's head as she tried to wrap her head around what she was hearing. She'd always thought, like everyone else, that the justices were there to support the crown and run their respective industries. She did not know how divided they were—and how little power Candace had. Plus, Candace was trying, in her own deluded way, to save all the queer people who were caught. Miriam's entire worldview was being flipped on its head, and she felt unstable. Shaky. This was all easier when Candace was just a villain.

"Why don't you stand up to them? Remind them who's boss?"

Candace laughed. "Half of them are looking for a reason to overthrow me. Plus, Alderman and Solomon Kingsley with Energy are wild cards. I can't tell if they hate me or love me."

"So, who does love you?" That was harsher than Miriam intended, and for a moment, Candace looked as if she'd been slapped. But she shook herself back to the expressionless face she used in public.

"Gideon Thomas and Noah Westcott support me." Transportation and Energy, Miriam recalled. Candace continued, "I've known Gideon since I was a little girl. He was good friends with my father. But kind."

But kind. What an interesting statement. Candace's father had been a violent ruler, and Miriam, along with everyone else in her circles, assumed Candace had followed suit.

Miriam shook her head. "You're telling me you have two reliable allies in the Supreme Court?"

Candace laughed. "Pitiful isn't it? And if they knew about—" she gestured toward Miriam "—everything, who knows if they'd still have my back."

Miriam's purpose was becoming clear. Candace lacked confidence, and she was the supposed ruler of the country. But maybe Miriam could convince her to stand up for herself, for the country. If she could assert her power, perhaps she could do some actual good.

There was a long silence as they both thought. Then Candace spoke, jolting Miriam from her plotting. "Well, where do you want me, Mistress?"

Miriam cocked her head. "Are you sure this is a good idea? You're upset and..."

"Please. I need this." The queen's eyes filled with tears. "I need it," she whispered again.

"Okay," Miriam agreed. Candace did need this, and Miriam needed to build this relationship so she could, in turn, build

Candace's confidence and convince her to start acting like the fucking absolute ruler she was. "Strip."

"Yes, Mistress." Candace's eyes lowered as she slipped into her submissive alter ego. She was well-trained, and Miriam gave a passing, curious thought about who her previous Dominant must have been. She wondered what happened to them.

"Are you familiar with the red, yellow, green method?" Miriam asked as she watched the queen strip down to nothing. Candace nodded. "Good. I expect you to use that with me. If you say red, I'll stop immediately. Understood?"

"Yes."

Miriam crossed the room and grabbed a fistful of Candace's dyed blonde hair. She tugged hard. "Yes, what?"

Candace whimpered. "Yes, Mistress."

"Good girl." Miriam gave one last hard pull, then released her. Candace stumbled, slipping down into a kneeling position. She dared a glance up at her Domme. "You're bratty today," Miriam said.

"No, Mistress."

Miriam recalled the yes-no-maybe list to determine her next steps. Candace had a humiliation kink and was a masochist. "Do you have a whip or anything?" That reminded her to ask about the MolecuMaker after their scene.

"Yes, Mistress. In my bedroom."

"Good. Show me. But crawl."

Candace obeyed. Miriam walked behind her as she slowly crawled, ass in the air, to her bedroom. She stopped in front of a large wardrobe. "In here, Mistress."

Curious and excited, Miriam opened the doors and found a decent collection of toys. Plenty to make a decent scene, and then some. Maybe they wouldn't need that MolecuMaker after all. Candace pointed at the floggers, whips, and paddles. "Those haven't been used in years."

She sounded sad. Miriam stooped and used two fingers to lift her chin. She gazed into the trusting blue eyes of the queen. "That ends today."

Candace breathed deeply and relaxed against Miriam's hand. "Yes, Mistress."

Miriam pulled out a hefty leather flogger and tested its weight. She missed her own collection of toys. A wave of nausea washed over her as she thought about her parents going through her apartment once they found out she was "dead." She pushed the thought away.

"Permission to speak freely, Mistress?"

God, she was so well-trained. "Yes, go ahead."

Candace placed her palms up in a placating gesture. "I wanted to apologize for trying to force you into a scene last time. And I don't expect these scenes to lead to sex, even though I hope they do at some point."

Miriam blinked. "Oh. Thank you. Uh, where did this come from?"

"I told Asher what happened, and he reamed my ass about it."

Interesting. But Miriam would take it.

"Let's just take it one step at a time for now, okay?" Miriam asked. Candace nodded, and Miriam arched a brow.

"Yes, Mistress."

"Good, now get on the bed. On your stomach."

Candace nearly leaped onto the oversized mattress in her excitement, and Miriam had to laugh. She may have a harem full of people to fuck, but she was desperate for a dominating hand. Someone skilled, and Miriam was definitely skilled.

"Red, yellow, green," she reminded Candace before sweeping the first light touch of the flogger's tips against Candace's thighs. Candace bobbed her head into the pillows.

The first few hits weren't hard, just enough to tease her skin. Candace was so pale that her skin turned pink already. "Harder, Mistress."

"I'll decide when you're ready for harder, Candace." She ran the tips of the flogger over the queen's ass and thighs, teasing her into misery. "Are you wet?"

"Ye-yes."

Thwack. A hard hit. Unexpected. Candace bucked. "Yes, Mistress," she breathed.

"Color?"

"Green! Mistress!"

Thwack. "Good girl. You know how to be a good girl, don't you?" Another hard hit, this time square on her left butt cheek. "But that's part of your problem."

Miriam grew wet as she watched Candace's skin turn red under the flogger's pummeling hits. She licked her lips. "You can be a good girl for me. But why do you want to be a good girl for those men? They don't respect you."

Candace whimpered and moaned. She raised her ass in the air, asking silently for more. Miriam obliged. She would be sore tomorrow, and most definitely sport a few purple bruises. Liquid dripped down Candace's inner thighs.

"Such a pain slut," Miriam murmured. She tossed the flogger aside and stepped closer to the bed. She gave a good smack with her hand, and Candace crumpled to the bed. A spank would sting on skin that inflamed. Miriam watched as Candace snaked a hand underneath her stomach toward her vulva.

Miriam spanked her again. "I didn't say you could touch yourself." Candace removed her hand and gripped the bedsheet. She tried to grind her hips against the bed, but Miriam placed a firm hand on her back.

"You little slut. You're so used to getting whatever you want. You need to learn some denial." Of course, this pain and submission was what she wanted. But someone had to control the sex fiend.

Miriam knelt on the bed next to Candace and wound her blond locks in her hand. She tugged hard and raised Candace's face. "You don't get to touch yourself. If you can come from the pain, then you can come." She stroked a hand down Candace's spine. "Where are you?"

"Green." Her face was streaked with tears, and her mouth curved in a gentle smile. "Please keep going, Mistress. It's been so long since I've felt like this. So long."

Well, she was still talking in full sentences, so she wasn't near subspace. Miriam looked at the fiery red on her skin. A couple of purplish bruises had already begun to form on her rear. She needed to be careful not to overwork her, but Candace had spirit and a hell of a masochistic streak.

Miriam used her hand instead of the flogger for the rest of the session. She peppered in a few hard hits with softer ones, ones that wouldn't bruise. But they stung, and soon Candace was moaning into the pillows. She collapsed from her knees onto her stomach, and her body went stiff as an orgasm washed over her. She quaked with aftershocks, and Miriam sat beside her as she came down from her high, watching and pondering how her entire life had changed in an instant.

She'd just finished a scene with a sometimes sub, a pretty redhead, and they came out of the club together. They were both giddy from the high of the scene, and two blocks away, they'd kissed. And they'd been caught. A cop had seen the whole thing, but Angel had insisted that Miriam had forced her. A lie to save herself, and Miriam couldn't even blame her. Not when the punishment was death—or so everyone believed.

But then Angel had done the unthinkable. Maybe she thought the cop was skeptical about her story, so she sealed the deal. Saved herself and told the cop that Miriam was Lady Lilith.

Years of hiding, of hard work, of being a beacon to the Depraved, over in an instant because of a stupid kiss.

"Mmm." Candace stirred next to Miriam and gave her a sleepy smile. "That was nice."

Miriam stroked a hand in the queen's hair, unable to stop herself from the sweet aftercare gesture. "Let me draw you a bath."

"Mmkay."

She found her way to the massive bathroom attached to Candace's bedroom. A huge circular tub stood in the middle of the pink marbled floor. God, she really loved pink.

Miriam turned the water on, found a button for jets, and located a bottle of bubble bath. Someday, she was going to use this. She'd never had the luxury of using bubble bath. Soap was already so expensive, and she hadn't had a bath since she was a kid. The Residence had nice showers, but no tub.

She spent some time sitting next to Candace as she bathed. She washed the queen's hair and hated herself for it. Candace was content not to talk, so other than a few murmurs that she did so well and was such a good girl, Miriam was quiet. Then she tucked her enemy—or maybe her ally—into bed and returned to cry in her small bedroom in the harem.

11

Asher's blood boiled as he made his way down to the Residence from Candace's office. How fucking dare Miriam! She'd barely been in the harem for two weeks, and she was already threatening everything he and Candace had worked for. Candace had managed to keep the peace with the Supreme Court for years now. But one session with Miriam, and she was rocking the boat. She'd told Pierce and Grant that they needed to provide shelter and medical care for the displaced neighborhood, or she would have their titles stripped. And she'd said it in front of the entire court of justices.

Candace was in tears because Pierce had laughed at her and Grant had told her that her crown wasn't safe. He was right, too. Candace could enact social laws and enforce them and was over intelligence. Of course, every division had their own military and intelligence. If the justices aligned, they could strip her of her power. Put in a puppet or do away with the monarchy altogether. Candace being queen was the only thing keeping the peace and keeping the Depraved safer than they were under her father's rule.

And Miriam had gone and told Candace to stand up to these evil, vile old men. She had no understanding of the shaky power dynamics that ran in the shadows of the Holy USA. If Candace wanted to keep her around for some pain play, he wasn't going to stand in the way. But he couldn't let her threaten the safety of the country.

He stormed into the Residence and took the stairs two at a time to Miriam's room. He'd start there, and he wouldn't stop until he told her what she needed to know. His pulse pounded in his ears as he made his way to the hallway of bedroom pods. Her door was ajar, and he didn't stop to knock.

"Miriam, we need to—Oh, Jesus Christ!"

Miriam looked at him in surprise from where she straddled someone in a mask on her bed. Was that Elijah? She made no effort to stop or cover herself, and in her defense, it was her room.

"Can I help you?" She rolled her hips, eliciting a moan from the man beneath her. Definitely Elijah—Asher would know that sound anywhere.

"Have you ever heard of shutting the damn door?" he said, although he couldn't take his eyes off of her. Her body was delicious, all soft curves, stomach lined with pale stretch marks that he just wanted to lick. His cock hardened, and he hoped she wouldn't notice.

"We didn't know it was open. So, can I help you or are you just here to watch?"

Asher forced himself to close his eyes. "We need to talk."

Miriam exhaled an exasperated breath. "Well, this is a buzzkill. Sorry, darling. We'll have to continue this another time." Asher heard the bed shift, then a warm body pushed past him out the door.

"Fuck you very much, Ash," Elijah said in a low voice as he left the room.

"You can open your eyes now."

Asher peeked through half-closed eyelids to find Miriam tying a green silk robe. He opened his eyes wider. Somehow, she looked just as sinful covered in the thin fabric as she did naked riding his best friend. He pushed his glasses up and pinched the bridge of his nose. "We need to talk."

"You said that. What is going on?"

He laid out what had occurred, per Candace's story, with the Supreme Court today. Miriam grinned. "Good for her."

"No! Not good for her!" He threw his hands up. "Do you understand what would happen if they acted against her?"

"Oh, I don't know. Maybe they'd destroy the housing of an entire neighborhood for their skyscrapers with 48 hours' notice, leaving thousands of people homeless and hungry." She let out a dry laugh. "Oh, wait. They already did that. And do that pretty fucking regularly."

"It would be so much worse. Do you remember what it was like when her father was still king? The murders that went unpunished, how it wasn't even safe to walk down the street."

"Maybe you've been here too long, but it's still not safe to walk down the street!" She shook her head. "Are you that fucking clueless? It is not safe out there already. Rapes, burglaries, murders—made all the worse by the corrupt cops and military forces. Have you ever had to buy antibiotics on the black market? Ever gone hungry because the stores were closed with no food left in them?"

He paused. He had been in the Residence for seven years now, ever since the king had died prematurely. And he'd been from a wealthy, well-connected family. He'd stayed well-concealed in the closet and had avoided any suspicions that would have landed him in conversion camp as a teen. Miriam had already mentioned that she knew Sherah from camp. He'd heard stories of the horrors that took place there.

"You worked for the government, though," he said.

She smiled sadly. "You think that made things easier? A digital archivist doesn't exactly make a fortune. I went hungry. I couldn't afford to go to the doctor. And I'm one of the lucky ones—I had stable work and my own place. In the slums, but it was my own."

Asher sighed. "I'm sorry, Miriam. Truly, I am. But the situation with the Supreme Court is tenuous on a good day. If Candace goes in rocking the boat..."

"Maybe the boat needs to be rocked, Asher." She took a step closer to him. "Maybe the status quo isn't working. She's the fucking queen. She has unlimited resources at her disposal."

Asher swallowed. Her hazel eyes were fierce and determined. She'd no doubt been through things that Asher couldn't imagine. "The Depraved. We have to keep them safe."

"Don't act like I don't care about my community!" Her voice raised to nearly a yell. "Don't tell *me* of all people that we have to keep them safe. I dedicated my life to keeping them safe!"

"You ran a website!"

"About avoiding the cops, avoiding disease, playing safely, consent. I spent my own money, when I had it, on black market condoms and birth control for the people in my community." Her eyes hardened. "I held the hands of women while they got illegal abortions because they were raped, sometimes by cops."

Asher swallowed hard. "I had no idea..."

"Exactly. You don't know me." She turned around, as if she were done with the conversation, then stopped. "And let's get one thing straight. I didn't make Candace do anything. She's her own person."

"I know, but—"

"No. And you'd have her deal with constant disrespect while those men keep everyone in this country in poverty and fear."

"Of course I don't want that, but there's no other way."

Miriam spun on her heels and glared at him. "There's always another way. Maybe you're too scared to think of it, but there's always another way."

"That's naïve," he said, but his heart wasn't in the fight anymore. He just didn't want to back down. Perhaps he was scared—scared of what would happen if Candace was stripped of her authority. Was that so wrong? He didn't think so. Candace had not been prepared to take on any power. Her father had kept her sheltered, despite Candace being his only heir. But Asher had a degree in political science with more concept of how things worked than Candace. Or so he'd thought—his education was lacking, and theory only went so far. Together, though, they'd kept the peace, or at least avoided civil war.

"I'm done with this conversation, Asher. Candace needs confidence, no matter what she does with it. Keep pulling her strings if you must, but leave me out of it."

He sighed and took a step closer to her. He loomed over her and said in a low voice, "You chose to be in it."

"I simply reminded Candace that she is the queen." She raised her head to meet his eyes. "What's the real issue here, Asher? Are you a coward, or do you not like Candace making her own decisions?"

The words pierced his gut. "Of course not." He was a coward, though. He knew that deep in his soul and remembered it every single day. "Candace is a grown woman."

"I don't think this is about Candace at all." Miriam blinked up at him.

"Oh? What is it about, then?"

"You're jealous of me."

"What? No!"

"You clearly don't like me. And you don't like that maybe Candace will listen to someone besides you."

Her robe slipped then, and Asher's eyes dropped to the exposed cleavage. His voice was husky as he said, "I like you plenty, Miriam. That's the problem."

She drew her fingertips over her collarbone and chest. "Why is that a problem?"

"Because I can't be with you, Miriam." He drew his gaze back to her beautiful, round face. "I can't give in."

A look of confusion flashed over her face, then surprise. "Give in? So you want me?"

"Miriam, if anyone doesn't want you, they're a fool." He ran a hand over his face. "Maybe I envy Candace and the others."

"You can have me." She placed her hand on his chest. "Say the word."

He sighed. "I can't, Miriam."

"Why?"

"It's complicated." He closed his eyes, took a deep, steadying breath, and reminded himself of the reason he had come here in the first place. "Tread carefully with Candace, please."

She shook her head. "No."

12

Asher washed himself in the large, marble-tiled shower, one of Candace's few over-the-top luxuries he truly enjoyed. He hadn't meant to linger for long, but the image of Miriam's naked body appeared unbidden in his mind. He remembered her gasp, the look of pure pleasure on her face as she threw her head back. The heat in her eyes when she realized he was watching.

His cock twitched, and his blood boiled in arousal, anger, jealousy, and shame. It should have been him underneath her, bringing her to ecstasy. But it couldn't be.

Deciding to take advantage of being alone, he left the hot water running and crossed the massive shower to take a seat on the stone bench. He let the steam lick his skin and imagined it to be the heat from her body. It took only a moment for him to grow hard, and he stroked himself in slow, languorous motions. He leaned his head back against the tile and closed his eyes.

As his strokes became faster, and his heart rate sped up, he heard the bathroom door opening and closing. Shit. He must have forgotten to lock it. He was just about to announce that the shower was occupied when he heard Miriam's voice ask, "Who left the water running?"

Asher froze. He should say something, should get up and

return to the stream of water from the showerhead and face the opposite wall. He should certainly let go of his erection. But he found himself unable to do any of those things. And when Miriam appeared at the edge of the shower in all her naked glory, that's how she found him. Panicked expression and hard cock in hand.

Her eyes widened as she realized she wasn't alone. Asher sat still as her gaze raked over his naked body, taking in his aroused state. When her stare focused on his erection, his heart thudded in his ears like thunder.

And then she licked her lips.

His hand moved of its own accord, and his mouth went dry. Miriam said nothing as she stepped inside the shower and let the water flow over her thick hair, her round shoulders, her luscious breasts. She washed herself, lathering shampoo into her hair. She closed her eyes and—damn her!—moaned as she worked the strawberry scent into her scalp. Asher watched, entranced, hardly aware of his hand on his shaft.

When her hair was clean, and Asher was hopelessly bewitched, she met his eyes and began soaping her body. Slowly. Deliberately. She bit her lip as Asher's hand pumped harder. His lips parted as she lathered her breasts and trailed the washcloth over the swell of her stomach. Her chest rose and fell faster as her breathing quickened, causing her breasts to bounce.

He squeezed himself to stave off the orgasm that bubbled just out of reach. If he came, he would have to stop watching. And he wasn't a strong enough man for that. The washcloth grazed the patch of dark hair that he dreamed about so often. He'd never envied a piece of fabric till now. And when that square of fabric breached the space hidden between Miriam's thighs,

Asher threw his head back and groaned.

When he opened them, Miriam knelt before him. Miriam, who knelt for no one. Miriam, who brought everyone to their knees in want of her.

Water droplets raced over her body. If he just reached his arm out, he could touch her. She lowered her head and raised her eyes, and the sight shook him to his core. A picture of her kneeling with a collar around her throat, her hands bound behind her in silk rope formed in his mind.

He shivered. "Fuck."

"Asher," she whispered, barely audible over the sound of the shower. "Asher, let me help you. Please."

He had never wanted anything more. But the picture of her submission was quickly replaced by a flash of painful memories.

"Fuck," he said again.

"Let me please you, Asher."

He reached out then and stroked her cheek. She closed her eyes at his feather-light touch. He trailed his fingers across her face and over her small, divine lips. Without warning, she took his fingers in her mouth and began to suck.

"Miriam." Her name came out half-prayer, half-beg. "I can't. I've told you."

She sucked harder and swirled her tongue around his fingertips. His hips bucked. He dropped the hand that had his cock in a vice grip, but did not remove the one from her mouth.She pulled her head back. He grieved the loss of her mouth. "You want it."

"Yes."

"You want me."

"Yes." There was no use denying that. Not now. "But..."

"You won't."

He shook his head. "I won't."

With sad eyes, she took his hand in hers and interlaced their fingers. Somehow, that simple gesture was more intimate than anything that had happened between them, and it sent him over the edge.

He came, spurting white over his chest and stomach. She squeezed his hand as he rode the high, guiding him through it. When he returned to himself, she stood. She gave him a sad smile and her washcloth, the same that he had envied for caressing the parts of her body he craved. Then she was gone. A few moments later, the bathroom door opened and closed again, leaving him alone with his regret and shame.

He studied the purple square of lush fibers, remembering the way it had washed over her, the way it breeched the secret between her thighs. Then he clutched it to his chest, feeling foolish. His spent cock stirred impossibly. A single tear ran down his cheek as he returned a hand to relieve himself once again.

Shame was always the other side of the coin from pleasure. This time, though, his shame hurt Miriam. Hating himself, he closed his eyes and stroked himself quickly to completion, imagining the pain on her face as she had left.

13

Miriam hadn't been able to stop thinking about the shower for two weeks now. She and Asher had tried their best to avoid each other, limiting their interactions to polite "good mornings" and "excuse mes." Her feelings were getting more complicated by the minute. Oh, she respected his rejection; she'd be an ass if she didn't. But she didn't understand why he rejected when he was just as into her as she was him. Was it because he thought Miriam was going to throw the country into civil war?

As far as that went, Miriam had become Candace's other confidante. She didn't tread carefully, as Asher had requested. She told Candace that she had a duty to her citizens, talked frankly about what life was like outside of the harem. Candace was less perky these days, only seeming truly happy during a scene. Good, Miriam thought. She needed to know that her people were hurting, starving, dying.

The queen's birthday was in two days, and she begged Miriam to make all her dreams come true. Apparently, the naughty thing had sneaked into some BDSM clubs in her younger days. She couldn't very well do that now. So, she asked Miriam to turn the Residence into a dungeon for the night. No matter that very few of the Residents had any kink experience.

Which is why Miriam found herself draping black cloths over the lights in the harem and arranging furniture for ease of scenes. Several of the others were going through the collection of toys, the ones from Candace's dresser and some that Isaac had designed for the MolecuMaker. She planned to go over the basics of consent and safety over dinner. The queen wanted everyone to participate, even if that only meant watching. So far, everyone was excited.

Everyone except Asher.

He watched the proceedings from a low red couch. A book rested in his hands; he'd apparently given up on trying to read, but she didn't know why he didn't just go somewhere else. She wondered if he was going to take part at all in the festivities. She kept sneaking pathetic glances at him as she decorated and placed bottles of lube on tables.

What a strange life she lived now.

"Oh, I've always wanted to try one of these," Abel said. Miriam glanced over to see him holding her personal favorite—a red leather flogger.

"You should practice," she offered. "I can show you how to use it later."

"It can't be that hard." Abel turned and looked at Marah. "Let me try this on you."

"Fuck no," Marah said. "Not my kink."

"What is your kink?" Jez asked curiously.

Marah shrugged. "I don't know. Still trying to figure that out."

Miriam sighed. She had work to do before Candace's birthday. At least she had two full days. Candace would be busy attending a parade in her honor tomorrow, so her party wouldn't take place until night.

Elijah cleared his throat. "I'll do it, Abel." Elijah had embraced his role as a submissive with glee. He needed anonymity, to feel less like a person. He'd also taken to bringing Miriam her coffee in the mornings. She didn't want to screw up their friendship by taking him on as a sub—she didn't feel that way about him. But she'd take the coffee if it scratched some service need of his.

"Excellent!" Abel said. "Uh, how do we start?"

Oh, God. This was going to be a disaster, and it could get dangerous. Miriam needed to keep an eye on things.

"I guess I'll lie down?" Elijah said, pulling his shirt off. He cleared off a bed-sized ottoman and lay down on his stomach, burying his head in his arms.

By this point, everyone was watching like it was Elijah's movie comeback. Even Asher had set aside his book entirely. Miriam plopped down on a chair with a good vantage point and folded her arms across her chest.

Abel grabbed the flogger in his fist, pulled his arm back too far, and before Miriam could react, landing a resounding smack straight across the small of Elijah's back.

Elijah yowled in pain. A few people exclaimed. And as Miriam jumped up and cried, "What the FUCK, Abel?" he landed another hard thud right under Elijah's lowest rib.

"Stop it!" Miriam cried.

Asher leapt up and grabbed the flogger from Abel. "Jesus, dude. You're going to do some damage." He knelt beside Elijah and asked, "Are you all right?"

Elijah nodded.

"That's not how it's supposed to feel, okay?"

He nodded again. "How is it supposed to feel?"

Asher sighed and stood, shaking his head. "First of all, you need to watch out for kidneys and these floating ribs." He drew his fingers over Elijah's back. "Got it, Abel?"

Abel looked sufficiently chastised. "Yes."

"Avoid the spine, especially the lower back where the tailbone is."

"I didn't mean to hit him there."

Miriam slowly sat back down, her eyes wide with surprise. Asher had this covered. She watched as he showed Abel how to hold the flogger between his fingers to limit his wrist motion. That was how Miriam held it, too.

"If they yell out in pain like that, you *have* to check in with them." Asher turned a stern gaze on Abel's face.

"But how do you know if it's a good yell or a bad yell?" Sherah asked from across the room.

Asher shrugged. "Practice. Just check in a lot, too much, until you get used to it. And make sure your bottom has a safe word."

"I always use red-yellow-green," Miriam added, and Asher nodded. She explained the meaning, though it was fairly obvious. Yellow confused some people, though, so she explained how a top needs to slow down and maybe change activities or areas.

"Now, back to the flogger," Asher continued. "You want to stand off to the side a little so you aren't having to cross your body with your arm. Otherwise, you'll tire too quickly."

He stood off to Elijah's left and peppered a few light hits across his upper back, careful to avoid the spine. "This warms the skin up, brings the blood to the surface. Don't go straight into the hard hits."

Miriam sat back. She couldn't take her eyes off his forearms. How had she not noticed how strong they were? He looked like a natural with the flogger, and a small part of Miriam wished she was the one on the ottoman. Of course, then she couldn't watch the show. A dull ache in her core formed, and she crossed her legs to abate the sensation, but only made it worse. Damn.

Asher demonstrated moving his body closer and further to vary how much leather was hitting the skin. Everyone was quiet, except for Elijah's soft moans and the sound of the smooth flogger slapping against his back.

"Tell me where you're at, Elijah." Asher's voice was low and gruff as he gave the command.

"I'm good. Green," he breathed.

Asher flogged him harder a few times. Miriam's gaze went down Asher's body, and her eyes stopped when she noticed a slight tenting of his pants. She licked her lips. Some sort of connection was being made in Miriam's mind, but Asher's perfect body and perfect Dominant form distracted her.

Eventually, he handed the flogger off to Abel and instructed him in a hushed voice. Miriam blinked as realization dawned on her. She nearly blurted it out but caught herself. Later, she would be talking to Asher because she had questions.

Over the next hour, Miriam and Asher taught the harem residents about several of the various items, like riding crops, silk rope, and whips. The handcuffs weren't popular, and Miriam realized they'd all been arrested before coming here. Well, maybe not Asher. She still didn't know his story, although she thought she was figuring it out.

Asher slipped away from the room and headed toward the staircase. Miriam followed him and stopped him outside their rooms. "Hey."

He sighed and turned around to face her. "Hey."

"You did good back there." She folded her arms. "You know your stuff."

"Say what you want to say, Miriam."

"You were her Dominant, weren't you?"

He swallowed, his Adam's apple bobbing. "Yes. I was."

"Then why aren't you now? Why did she need a Dominant so badly?"

He closed his eyes. "Because I don't do that anymore."

"Kink?"

"Any of it," he said in a harsh whisper. "Kink, sex, relationships. I don't do any of it."

Miriam's eyes widened. "You don't have sex with Candace? But everyone thinks..."

"I know what everyone thinks." He opened his eyes and closed the few feet of distance between them. He leaned down and brought his face closer to hers. "I don't see the point in correcting them. It would be weird if I lived in the harem and didn't service Her Majesty like everyone else, wouldn't it?"

"Why are you here, then?"

His eyes hooded. "There's nowhere else for me to go. And you know what?"

"What?" She stepped even closer. Her breasts nearly grazed his chest, and his gaze slipped lower. She took a deep breath and tried to resist reaching out and touching him.

"I was doing just fine before you showed up." He ran his fingers through her hair and inhaled her scent. Miriam closed her eyes against his touch. They stood like that for a few moments, and then Asher stepped back.

Miriam understood. Whatever haunted him ran too deep for her to solve. He would have to work it out on his own and only if he wanted to. She cleared her throat.

"Candace is going to want me to participate, so I can't keep an eye on everyone. Namely Abel. You should be the dungeon master."

He froze then jerked his head in a short nod. "Okay. I can do that."

14

Somehow, Miriam had pulled it off. She'd turned the main room of the Residence into a dungeon. The lights were low, and the furniture was arranged in a circle, so everyone would have a clear vantage point of the activities. On tables, various toys, restraints, and blindfolds lay waiting for play. Next to the largest sofa stood a full-sized St. Andrew's cross. How the hell Miriam had managed that, Asher had no idea. Isaac had mentioned something about the large MolecuMaker, but that sort of hacking was beyond his limited skill set.

Asher had even dressed for the occasion. He sported an old pair of leather pants, leather boots, and an open leather vest that bared his chest. He'd borrowed eyeliner from Sherah. Candace fucking owed him, but this is what she wanted. And being dungeon master for the evening meant that he didn't have to actively participate.

But oh, how he wanted to participate. Holding that flogger in his hand had awakened something he thought was dead. Something he wished was dead. For the first time in years, he'd felt completely in control of himself. And the way Miriam had watched him…his cock stirred just thinking about the way she'd licked her lips.

He hadn't even felt ashamed that everyone could see how

aroused he'd been. Well, until later. The shame always came later, but it was subdued. It hadn't torn at his soul; more like, it had shown up because it had to. Because, without shame, Asher didn't know who he was.

Some of the harem residents trickled in, all in varying states of undress. Clearly, everyone had visited the wardrobe generator for this event. The air buzzed with anticipation and excitement. As far as he knew, only Esther had ever visited a BDSM club before her arrest. This was new to almost everyone.

He knew the moment Miriam entered the room without even turning around. Everyone froze and turned toward the stairs. Asher spun around and stared at the knee-high stiletto leather boots that accentuated the soft curves of her calves. An expanse of pale skin rose from her knee to the bottom of a red leather mini-skirt. If she moved just right, Asher knew he'd be able to see everything, and he wanted that more than anything. He salivated. Her bodice was red and black leather with intricate straps across the front. Her ample breasts nearly spilled over the top. She'd painted her lips black as sin.

But what arrested him most was the way she caught his eye and gaped. Her gaze swept over him and her breasts heaved as she took a deep breath. He smirked at her, pleased he could do to her what she did to him.

Miriam cleared her throat. "I'm going to fetch Candace. Can someone start the music?" Jez hurried over to the large tablet on the wall and pressed play. Low beats filled the room from the speakers.

"You look incredible, Miriam," Sherah said. Asher glanced around the room and saw that everyone was still mesmerized. Candace might be the queen of the country, but it was clear who was in command tonight.

"It's Lilith tonight. Or Mistress." She descended the rest of the stairs. "Remember, no one has to do anything they don't want to do. And voyeurism is still a kink." She looked at Asher. "Asher will be your dungeon master tonight. Anything happens, you talk to him."

"Safe, sane, and consensual," Asher said, looking at Abel. "Remember that."

The doors opened and Asher turned his head to watch Miriam's round ass bounce in her miniskirt as she left the Residence and headed toward the elevator. She'd be back soon, and the party would begin. But Jez and Esther were already making out on one side of the room. Elijah, in a full gimp suit, knelt at Isaac's feet as Isaac tested a whip in the air.

A few minutes later, the doors opened again, and it was Asher's turn to gape. Candace wore a black mini-dress with no sleeves. She looked beautiful next to her mistress, but that wasn't what caught Asher by surprise. No, the queen wore a leather collar attached to a short red leash. Miriam held it loosely in one hand, whispered something in Candace's ear, and tugged.

Asher heard a quiet, "Yes, Mistress," as Candace sank to her hands and knees. Miriam walked with ease in her stiletto boots as she pulled Candace along behind her. Candace had a soft smile on her face. Asher had never been one to be submissive, but he envied Candace with his whole being right then. He would gladly follow Miriam on his hands and knees, and judging by the expression on everyone else's face, so would they.

Miriam was a goddess. If goddesses came clad in leather. It

was obvious why she had such a strong reputation among the Depraved. Lady Lilith was divine.

She lashed Candace to the St. Andrew's cross. She chose a riding crop first, and soon the sound of smacked flesh blended with the electronic drumbeats of the music. It was the sign to begin, and Asher slipped into his role. He kept his eyes keen in the lowlight, taking in the scene.

Sherah, clad in a latex dress, had opted for a blindfold as Daniel knelt before her and ate her out. Abel was balls deep in Marah, fucking her from behind and pulling her hair. Esther, Jez, and Elijah took turns laving over Isaac's thick, brown cock.

This was far from Asher's first dungeon orgy. He'd been to many, had trained under a Domme at the most popular underground club in the capital. But he'd never been more aroused than he was now. And for once, he was in the moment, not lost to dark thoughts that came unbidden, like a high-speed train. No, he was present here, among the people he knew best in life—and after tonight, would know even better.

Grunts and moans filled the air as pairs became trios and lovers switched. Whips cracked, flesh smacked, and wet noises of fucking surged straight to Asher's cock.

Candace was enjoying herself. She'd discarded her dress and wore only the collar and leash and a pair of nipple clamps that Abel tugged on. Marah had joined the group with Jez and Isaac.

And Miriam...fuck. She had her fingers on one hand in Candace's mouth, while her other hand had disappeared under her skirt. It was too dark to see her fuck herself, but Asher drew closer anyway. She was magnetic, and he needed to be near her. Those should be his fingers making her come undone.

She met his eye as he stood over her. He could hear the wet

sounds of her pussy, her mewls of pleasure. The heady scent of sex in the room tickled his nose.

"See something you like?" she whispered.

"You know I do."

"Why don't you join me?"

Asher was so close to bending down and replacing her hand with his own. So close to pulling her into his lap and bringing her screaming to orgasm. But just as he began to lean over, someone behind him said, "Yellow."

He straightened abruptly and turned to find Jez on the cross. Thankfully, Daniel backed off and lowered the whip in his hand. He smoothed his hand over Jez's still-clothed body. Everything was fine, but the moment was over. Asher remembered what his responsibility was tonight, and what he deserved every day. Miriam had pulled him under her spell, and and he nearly forsook his vows.

The rest of the evening passed without incident, but Asher was distracted and angry at himself. He had no one to blame but himself for his near lapse in judgment. People left to their beds or someone else's. Candace was deep in sub-space, her eyes glossy and happy as Miriam led her back upstairs.

Soon Asher was alone in the main room. He slumped onto a couch, closed his eyes, and pulled out his cock. It had strained against the leather all night, and it took him only a few strokes to climax.

He came with Miriam's name on his lips.

15

Miriam floated on her back in the warm pool, eyes closed, trying to get the image of Asher out of her brain. Asher in leather pants. Asher wielding a flogger. Asher in fucking eyeliner.

"Argh!" she exclaimed, then opened her eyes to make sure she was alone. Isaac had paused on his way to the workout room, his brow raised in confusion.

"I'm fine!" Miriam promised and waved him off. Sighing, she swam toward the side of the saltwater pool, as the water wasn't helping her to relax and get Asher out of her mind. She had barely slept a wink, thinking of what she had heard as she re-entered the harem the night before. Her obsession, this thing between them—it was getting out of hand.

She pulled herself from the pool, adjusting the bottom of her bikini. Memphis had banned bikinis, and she'd always wanted to wear one. Now she could do whatever she wanted within the confines of the harem walls. She pressed her wet hands against her eyes; she was yet to find some sort of hobby here to keep her occupied. Knitting wasn't it. Neither was cooking, despite her best attempts. Reading was nice, but eventually her mind would wander...to her captivity, to her parents, to the Supreme Court and Candace.

To Asher.

Despite her best attempts, she was obsessed with him. She wasn't looking for love. Never had, never would. But her attraction to Asher was starting to feel a lot like, well, feelings. Clearly, she just needed to scratch the itch and get him out of her system.

She wrung the water out of her hair and wrapped the oversized towel around herself. She'd had to use Candace's generator to make towels that fit well around her ample figure, and they were cozy and soft, the complete opposite of what she felt right now. Once she was dry enough, she made her way to the stairs toward her room. When she got to the top, Asher was heading to the staircase. He flashed a grin at her. "Good swim?"

"Yeah." She paused, and the silence between them felt charged. "Hey, about last night…"

He straightened and sucked in a breath. "Last night was a lapse in my judgment."

Miriam was tired of this. His avoidance made her feel dirty, shameful, and she'd be damned if she let anyone make her feel that way.

"Am I so repulsive?" Even as she said it, she knew the words weren't true.

"What? No! God, no, Miriam." He took a step toward her, reached out a hand, then stopped. "No. It has nothing to do with you."

"Then please, tell me what it does have to do with. Because this dance between us is driving me crazy."

Asher closed his eyes. "My sister."

Miriam blinked. That was not the response she was expecting. "You—you have a sister?"

He replied in a monotone voice, "I did. And she's dead because of me." He opened his eyes, his brown orbs boring into her soul. "It's…"

Understanding dawned on Miriam. "So, this life here in the harem, this is your penance?"

He ran a hand over his face. "I can't let myself forget."

"How long?" She closed the distance between them and took his hand in hers.

"Eight years now."

"That's a long time." She squeezed his hand. "I still don't understand what it has to do with us."

"Miriam, I can't…"

"I heard you last night!" She hadn't meant to say it, but now that it was out…"When I came back downstairs, and you were on the couch."

Asher's eyes darkened, but he said nothing.

"You said my name as you came." She took a step closer. "You want this as bad as I do."

"I can't give you what you want, Miriam," he whispered. She arched her neck and met his gaze.

"I'm not looking for love, Asher. Just sex."

Without warning, he grabbed her and backed her against the nearest wall, pinning her arms above her head in one strong hand. "Is this what you want? I'm a monster, Miriam. You don't want me."

Monster? Miriam blinked. What was he talking about? And if he was trying to scare her, this was the wrong way to go about it. She raised her chin toward him, challenging. His eyes were hooded, his breathing heavy. His free hand roamed up the side of Miriam's body, gracing her with an incendiary touch. She gasped as he stole across the curve of her breast.

"You don't want me," he repeated in a low voice. Still holding her arms above her head—God, he was tall—his roaming hand came up and covered her throat. He applied no pressure. They stood there, holding each other's gaze, the only sound their rapid breaths. Their bodies pressed against one another. With only a towel around her, Miriam could feel his erection.

She pressed her neck forward. "Do it," she whispered. He squeezed lightly, not even enough to hitch her breath. She moaned and rolled her hips, letting him know just how much she wanted this.

He moved his hand and pushed a wet lock of hair away from Miriam's ear. He leaned down and whispered in her ear. "Miriam...what you do to me..."

His lips captured her earlobe, and he nibbled. Miriam strained against him, but he did not release her arms. She was his captive. Heart racing with a spike of fear at the powerlessness, she breathed his name.

That seemed to wake him. His lips descended on hers with a scorching ferocity. Finally, finally, he dropped her arms and pulled her even closer to him. Her arms wound around him, exploring the tight muscles of his back as he plundered her mouth. This was no gentle, romantic kiss. His tongue was strong and needy. His teeth nipped at her lips, and she dug her fingers into his hair.

She groaned, half in frustration, as he still wasn't close enough, though their bodies were intertwined. She hiked a leg up around his waist and pressed his erection against the damp bottoms of her swimsuit. He growled and rutted against her, his lips never stopping the assault on her mouth. She ran her nails down his back and onto his ass. He returned the favor by yanking her hair.

"Take me," she breathed.

Grasping her wrist, he all but dragged her down the hallway toward their bedroom pods. The towel around her fell, and neither of them stopped to pick it up. He paused between their rooms, brow furrowed for the briefest moment, then tugged her toward her door. Miriam let the retinal lock scan her eyes, and the door slid open. In seconds, he had pushed her down on the bed, then straddled her before stealing her lips again.

She tugged at his shirt, and he broke the kiss just long enough to pull it over his head. He fumbled with the strings of her bikini top. "This barely covers anything," he said with a laugh.

"For your enjoyment," she replied. Once the strings were free, her breasts were bare, and she pulled him against her with a moan. His chest was toned, his puckered nipples light brown. Miriam grazed a nail over one of them, making Asher suck in a breath.

"Minx."

He lowered his head and burrowed his face between Miriam's breasts. He alternated biting and kissing his way between them and over her stomach. Then his tongue licked up her abdomen all the way to her neck. She arched off the bed, but his hips kept her pinned down. She scratched him, hard, and he swore before pulling one of her nipples into his mouth.

"Fuck!" she cried. He sucked and nipped until she was bucking against him. God, she needed him to touch her, to let her find release already. But as his head moved to her other breast, she knew he was going to take his time in torturing her.

16

Kissing Miriam was like communion. He felt it in the depths of his soul. She was fire and strength and all the good things in the world, and he wanted to devour it, devour her, until he was no longer broken.

Her damp hair splayed out underneath her on the bed, and he took a moment to gaze at her beauty. Her breasts were full and ripe and peppered with bites, and her rosy nipples had turned red beneath his mouth's worship. She was perfect.

The only thing still in the way were those damn bikini bottoms. He'd admired them on her round ass several times, but now he just wanted them gone. He hooked his fingers in the sides and yanked them down, exposing the patch of dark hair between her legs. Oh, he'd seen this before, but he'd never allowed himself to touch the treasure. But now? Now he was going to get this unbearable obsession out of his system. Maybe her presence would stop tormenting his dreams if he just allowed himself to a taste of her.

"Get your damn clothes off," she ordered him. He cocked a brow, but she met his expression with her own indignant look. He'd never allowed someone to order him around in the bedroom before, other than when he apprenticed to become a Dom. Honestly, he'd never been into it, but when Miriam gave the orders...well, how could he refuse?

He disrobed, then crawled on top of her again, capturing her mouth in another searing kiss. Her tongue fought his for dominance. He bit her lip, not gently, and she cried out. He pulled away. "Are you okay?"

She took advantage of the distance and pushed on his shoulders until he lay flat on the bed, then she straddled his abdomen. Oh, she'd pay for this switch in power, but the way her wet, leaking cunt felt against his stomach made him in no hurry to change their positions.

"Let's get something straight," she said. Her breaths came heavy, and her breasts heaved. "I will tell you if I'm not okay. I'm a big girl, Asher."

He swallowed and met her intense stare. It had been so long. What if he took things too far? But if he wanted her—and he did—he had no choice but to trust her. The thought terrified him.

But he nodded his understanding, and a huge grin lit up her face. "Christ, Asher, I've been thinking about this for weeks." She ran a hand over her tits and down to the space between her legs.

He caught her wrist. "That's mine."

"Bastard. I'm not yours."

He shook his head. "That delicious pussy is, though." He paused and decided to soften his meaning. "For tonight."

Miriam giggled and turned her head to the Moses Tablet on the wall. "It's only one o'clock."

Even he couldn't resist a smirk. Time moved differently in the harem, and he used to have to have all his rendezvous after dark. "Worried you can't go all night?"

She yanked her hand free of his wrist, and he reached behind her to swat her on the ass. "Don't underestimate me."

"I wouldn't dream of it," he replied honestly. Miriam was impossible to underestimate. She had a presence that demanded awe and respect. She was fierce and brave. And smart—how she had avoided capture as Lilith for so long, he had no idea. Damn him, he was starting to feel things for her, more than lust, and he needed to tread carefully. He couldn't give her more than this, and he shouldn't even be doing that.

He felt her hand caress his face. He'd gotten lost in thought, so he shook himself and smiled up at her from where she straddled him. "Now, get up here and let me eat that beautiful pussy."

She rearranged herself and scooted up to place her knees on either side of his head. Asher was quite certain his aching cock had never been harder in its life. Wrapping his arms around her thighs, he tugged her lower toward his eager mouth. He ran his tongue from her opening to her clit in one big swipe, and she bucked her hips.

"Fuck! Yes!"

He chuckled beneath her and breathed in her sweet scent. Careful not to give her exactly what she wanted, he began to lick in small, gentle movements. If there was one thing Asher had excelled in before he swore off sex, it was giving head—to anybody. It didn't take him long to settle into the familiar action.

God, she tasted heavenly, like salt from the pool and a hint of something sweet. He buried his tongue inside her as deep as he could. Miriam grabbed at his hair and rolled her hips. He squeezed her thick thighs, urging her to ride his face. Stopping whenever she began to clench, he smiled beneath her as he edged her closer and closer to orgasm. She swore at him, calling him names every time, but she moved her hips faster, coming undone.

Finally, he let her come with his tongue swirling furiously on her clit. She came with a loud cry, and Asher drank her up like the communion she was. But he didn't stop as her trembles became small aftershocks. Instead, he continued his ministrations, and it didn't take long for her to cry out his name. She came harder this time. Her hands tweaking her nipples as she ground against Asher's mouth was the most erotic thing he'd ever witnessed.

She climbed off his face. Sweat gleamed on her skin. "I'm not done with you yet," he growled.

"You fucking better not be."

She stretched out alongside him on the bed and pulled his face to hers, then licked off her own wetness from his chin before delving her tongue deep into his mouth. Her hand skimmed down his abs and circled the base of his leaking cock. He moaned.

"Such a perfect cock," she murmured against his neck. Then she pumped him as she sucked and bit right on his collarbone. He would have a visible hickey tomorrow. Everyone would give him shit about it, and he couldn't find it in himself to care. He wanted her to mark him. To claim him.

She was too good with her hands, and Asher's control was hanging on by a thread. As she lowered her head and planted kisses on his stomach, he caught her chin in his hand as she reached the top of his pubic area. She glanced up, her hair torturously brushing his oversensitive shaft, and smirked at him.

"I need to be inside of you."

She climbed back up toward him. "And how do you want me?"

Oh, he wanted her in every way. He thought for a moment as he grazed his hand over her cheek. With her on top, her tits bouncing gloriously? Or from behind, so he could squeeze and smack that round ass? Later. He'd already promised her the whole night. And deep down, he wanted to gaze into her eyes as he fucked her, to let her know who was in charge here, and to see her pretty face as she came around him.

He pushed her onto her back. Kneeling between her legs, he pulled her hips toward him, and she let out a squeal of surprise. She wrapped her legs around him and pulled him closer. He took his cock in his hand and ran it through her slickness before notching it at her entrance.

She was so wet, and he slid inside her with ease. He froze, trying not to come on the spot. Her tight heat had him in a vice grip, and oh, it had been so, so long. But he was determined to make this good for both of them. He squeezed his eyes shut for a moment, then started to move.

Her legs tightened around his waist. One foot digging into the small of his back, she urged him deeper. His thighs shook with his restraint.

"Harder," she demanded, and that was all he needed to let go.

His hips snapped as he fucked her deeply, roughly. Her eyes were closed, and her back arched as he plowed her with hard, short strokes. "Open your eyes. Look at me while I fuck you."

To his surprise, she obeyed him. He grabbed one of her legs and threw it over his shoulder so he could get a deeper angle.

She met his gaze, and tears leaked from the corners of her eyes as she panted and groaned beneath him. He felt her squeeze her inner muscles, making her hole impossibly tighter. He swore and laughed. When was the last time he had felt this happy?

Asher was wrong before. Miriam wasn't communion. She was baptism. She washed through the cavern of his soul, purging the darkness. He surrendered everything to her, and after this moment, he would rise from between her legs a sanctified man.

She came with a loud, "Fuck!" Her inner muscles tightened some more, and Asher was gone. Gone from himself, from the shadows that he carried with him. He pulled himself from her and came, spurting white over her belly, claiming her as his. He groaned as his ejaculation tore through him until he was utterly spent.

Collapsing onto the bed next to Miriam, he pulled her close under his arm. She gasped as she caught her breath. He combed his fingers through her hair as he lay there, waiting for the shame to show up. For the image of his sister's face to appear in his mind.

To his surprise, nothing was there except a sense of peace and the urge to laugh. It began as an embarrassing sort of giggle, which then caused Miriam to giggle. Then she snorted, which resulted in a loud guffaw from Asher. They held each other as they laughed. Tears pricked Asher's eyes, for once not caused by grief and despair.

He had fully intended to break his vow to himself with the knowledge that regret would be waiting on the other end. Instead, he felt nothing but happy.

17

Miriam stood in the kitchen, staring at the MolecuMaker as it brewed her coffee with creamer. Asher had his arms wrapped around her waist, and he nuzzled her neck with his chin. She sighed and leaned further back into his embrace. She never would have thought Asher to be so affectionate, but he couldn't seem to stop touching her. Probably touch-starved, she realized sadly.

They had fucked all afternoon and into the night, their sessions of lovemaking interspersed with talking and naps. Miriam was the best sort of exhausted this morning—there was no better reason to lose sleep than incredible sex. And it was incredible. With their chemistry, she'd known it would be. Although they both considered themselves Dominants, the back and forth taking and relinquishing of power had made them insatiable.

But she wondered what had changed in Asher, what had finally caused him to stop fighting their chemistry and take her to bed. And what had kept him from doing it weeks ago? She still didn't understand the darkness enveloping him, what kept him celibate in a literal harem. She'd expected him to pull away in the morning, to leave her alone in bed and withdraw back into himself. He hadn't, though, and that gave her a glimmer of hope. She could no longer deny her feelings for him, and she wanted to know all of him. Not just the part that gave her mind-blowing multiple orgasms.

She grabbed her coffee from the machine in the wall and spun around to face him. "Hey, can I ask you a question?"

It was a risk, she knew. He could go dark on her, pull away. But maybe after what they had shared last night...

"What's up?"

She took a deep breath and hoisted herself up on the kitchen island. "Will you tell me your story? Why you've sworn off sex until now?"

Asher leaned against the cabinets opposite her. Fixing her with his brown gaze, he thought for several moments. But his face hadn't shuttered, so Miriam waited, holding her breath.

"I can't..." He folded his arms. His shoulders hunched inward. "Only Candace knows the whole story. I don't think...I don't think I can get the whole thing out."

Miriam softened her expression and waited for him to continue. She would take whatever he would give her.

Asher sighed. He shook his leg in a nervous tic. "I'm...responsible for the death of my younger sister."

Whatever Miriam had thought he would say, that was not it. She noticed he didn't say he'd killed her, though.

He broke her gaze for the first time and studied the marble tile on the floor. Miriam didn't know if he would offer anything else. She was just about to change the subject when he spoke again. "I did something bad. With Candace. And it...well, through a series of events, my sister ended up dead."

When he raised his head again, tears brimmed in his big brown eyes. "It's too hard to explain. Maybe one day."

Miriam nodded in understanding. Her heart leapt at his promise of maybe one day, though. Perhaps what they had could last. He had to learn to trust her, and he'd taken the first steps last night. She supposed she could get the full story from Candace, but she didn't want to violate Asher's trust. It would just take time.

"Tell me something about you," he said.

"Me? I'm an open book." She shrugged and hoisted herself onto the countertop. "What do you want to know?"

He watched her as she took a sip of her coffee, a small smile on his face. She blushed into her mug. "Tell me about your parents. Were you close?"

She froze with her coffee mug halfway to her mouth. God, she thought about her parents more and more lately. By now, they had to know she was dead, or at least dead to the world. It was cruel, not letting the Depraved say goodbye to their loved ones, but Miriam supposed the secret would fall apart. Still, she wished she could tell them she was okay.

"I wouldn't say we were close, no. They were good parents, and I had a pretty good childhood. Our relationship is...was...fairly superficial, but I called home every couple weeks and made a point to see them every two months or so." Tears threatened to fall from her eyes, and she blinked them away. "I wish I had been a better daughter."

He took two steps forward and rested a hand on her knee. "I'm sorry. Sorry you're stuck here instead of out there making a difference."

"Let's change the subject," she said.

"Okay. To what?"

She forced a smirk on her face. "Sex, of course. Last night

was…"

"Incredible? Mind-blowing? Divine?"

She laughed, not having to fake it. "You think highly of yourself."

"I think highly of *you*." He placed a chaste kiss on her lips. "You want to know what I think?"

"What?" She set her mug down beside her and wrapped her arms around Asher's neck.

"I don't think you're as dominant as you let on."

"I think you're jealous and don't know what to do when you're not in charge."

"Oh, I was in charge." He leaned his forehead against hers. "At least some of the time."

She couldn't argue with that. Their ever-shifting power dynamic had been part of the fun. But Asher had a point, had realized something about her that she'd never told anyone.

"Sometimes," she whispered, "I wish I could sub for someone. But I don't trust anyone like that. I only trust myself. And honestly, it terrifies me."

He stood between her legs, which dangled off the countertop. Her breath hitched as he leaned in. He brushed his lips across hers, a feather-light touch, then grazed them along her cheek to her ear. He bit her earlobe, hard enough to make her gasp.

His breath was warm and wet on her ear. He whispered in a husky voice, "It scares you because you've created your own prison. A perfectly wound spool of control. Tight enough that you're afraid if it frays just a bit, everything will spiral. You're always in control because then you're not weak. Not vulnerable."

She shivered, whether from arousal or his keen, unsettling,

accurate assessment.

"But you crave it," he continued. He ran his hand up her back and wound it in her hair. "Because you want that release. You want to lose control. Lose yourself. Let someone else guide you and tell you what to do."

He yanked her hair hard enough to turn her head to the ceiling. She moaned instead of yelping from the unexpected pain. He nipped at her exposed throat.

"You want to feel something tangible. A real pain instead of that soul-searing pain wrapped inside that thread." She could only pant in response. "You need it."

His hand released its grip on her hair and swept over to her neck. Her scalp still stung as he placed his hand softly on her neck. He didn't squeeze, didn't even apply pressure. But he positioned his hand in a way that Miriam knew he knew what he was doing. Safe. Sane.

She squirmed beneath him.

Consensual.

"You need it," he repeated. He squeezed then. Miriam could still breathe, though it was harder. She met his deep brown eyes to find them nearly black, with his pupils blown in arousal.

It took some effort, but she formed the word, hating herself a little as it left her lips.

"Yes."

He released her, and her hands went straight to her throat. She'd never let anyone do that to her, but she found she was beginning to trust him. That was perhaps the most terrifying bit of all. She'd spent years relying on herself for everything, for her very safety. She didn't know how he'd made such an accurate assessment of her character with their limited interactions, but she knew he was observant. Watchful. And it was true that Miriam was more than a bit of a control freak.

Damn, he was good. She licked her lips, then used her legs to urge him closer to her. Her kiss was frantic and messy, but she needed it to convey what she couldn't say. What she couldn't even form in her mind.

He kissed her back, his hands running up her sides and into her loose hair. She couldn't give him complete control, though, not even after all that. Their kiss became the delightful push-and-pull that their lovemaking had been. Wetness pooled between Miriam's legs. She should be tired of sex, but something about Asher made her just want to never stop. He was addictive. Broody and dominant. Rough but gentle. If she wasn't careful, she would fall head over heels for him. Maybe she'd already begun.

A voice broke them from their passion. "Hey, not in the kitchen, y'all."

Asher and Miriam pulled apart and found Jez standing in the doorway. "Sorry," Miriam muttered.

"While we're all thrilled that you got over whatever shit was between you and fucked—loudly, all night, I might add—can you not do it where we make food?"

Asher blushed, red twinging his cheeks, and Miriam thought it was the most adorable thing she'd ever seen. "You're right, Jez," he said. "It won't happen again.

They rolled their eyes at the couple, then continued. "I do hate to interrupt. But Candace is requesting access to the harem. Says she needs to meet with all of us."

"Probably going to request a weekly dungeon party or some shit," Miriam muttered.

Jez shook their head. "I don't think so. This sounds serious."

Asher straightened. "What's going on?" If Asher didn't know, then it had to be urgent. Of course, he might have missed a summons from Candace since they'd been otherwise busy all night.

Jez shrugged. "I don't know. But she was crying."

Miriam gave Asher an alarmed look. "She was fine yesterday." Before her swim and subsequent run-in with Asher, Miriam had gone to check on Candace, to make sure she wasn't experiencing sub drop. But Candace had been floaty and giggly. Perhaps Miriam should have gone up one more time, but then she'd fallen in bed with Asher. Shit. She hoped this wasn't a delayed drop. The dungeon party had been intense, and Miriam would feel like shit if she hadn't taken care of her sub.

"Let's go." Concern laced Asher's voice. They followed Jez into the main living area of the Residence, and Asher took Miriam's hand in his. He gave it a light squeeze. "I'm sure it's fine," he said in a low voice that didn't sound convincing at all.

A pit formed in Miriam's stomach. Something felt off as they entered the room. Everyone was quiet, except for the sniffles from Candace. She stood near the door, as if she was ready to escape at any moment. Asher sat on a low sofa and pulled Miriam down next to him. She wasn't used to so much affection, and tensed.

"Everyone's here," Isaac said. "What's up, Candy?"

Miriam watched as Candace took a deep breath and tried to put on her queenly demeanor. She was shaking, and her eyes were puffy and red. Discontent swirled in Miriam's gut.

"There are..." Candace's voice broke. "There are riots."

Everyone looked around at everyone else, confused. No one

said anything and instead waited for Candace to continue. When she didn't, Asher was the first to speak up.

"What do you mean, 'there are riots?' Where?"

Candace closed her eyes. Her voice was a whisper. "Everywhere."

"Candy, you've got to give us more than that. Get it together." His voice was stern, and several people looked at him, surprised. Miriam realized most of the harem residents didn't truly understand that his role with Candace was advisor and friend. Even Miriam was a little taken aback at the harshness of his words.

"Why don't you sit down, Candace?" Miriam offered and gestured at an open seat. Candace nodded jerkily and made her way to sit down. She collapsed onto the low chair and buried her head in her hands.

"They started in Memphis," the queen said, her voice muffled.

Miriam inhaled sharply. Memphis was home. Did that mean...?

Candace looked up and met Miriam's eyes. "You have a very loyal community."

"Oh God." Faces of Miriam's beloved friends and lovers flashed in her mind. Riots meant violence. Death. Bile rose in her throat, and she grabbed onto Asher's arms in panic. She never wanted to be a martyr. She never wanted to bring anyone down with her. And now, her fake death had caused a riot.

"Once it got out that you were Lady Lilith, and that Memphis was protesting, the riots started in other cities. Dallas, Manhattan, Atlanta...it seems there are more every hour."

"When did this start?" Jez asked.

Candace buried her head again. "Two nights ago. But I just found out." Her blonde head shook. "I refused a news brief yesterday."

Two nights ago. The queen's birthday. While they were all flogging and fucking. Miriam was going to be sick.

After several minutes of silence, the queen finally sat back and assumed her role as leader. "I don't know much yet. I've dispatched intelligence. But these seem well-organized, especially Memphis. Like they've been waiting for the right moment for a long time."

"They have," Jez said. Everyone's head snapped to them. Jez was normally so reserved. It wasn't like them to be speaking up so much. "The people have been discontented for a long time."

Candace's eyes narrowed. "What do you know?"

Jez raised their hands in defense. "I've been in here for two years, Candace. I know nothing more than you. All I know is that people have been talking about a revolution for years."

They weren't wrong, but Miriam didn't run in political activist circles. She preferred her activism to stay anonymous and online and focused on sex. People muttered about wishing things were different, about overturning the government, but they had never seemed serious.

"A revolution?" Sherah said. "Is that what this is?"

Candace rubbed a hand over her eyes.

"How big are these riots?" Asher asked.

"Big enough that the cops can't get them under control," Candace replied. "The prisons are already overrun with protestors. In Memphis, rioters stormed one of the jails."

Miriam swallowed, not wanting to ask her question. But she steeled herself. "Are they using lethal force?"

Candace inclined her head in assent. "Both sides are. The rioters have weapons, too."

"You have to get this under control, Candace," Asher said. "We don't have the allies for a revolution. Not with Alderman and Defense as a wild card."

Miriam snapped her head toward him. "What do you mean, 'under control'?"

"It needs to be shut down." He tried to take Miriam's hand, and she jerked it away. Hurt flashed in his eyes. "Don't you see? This will be a bloodbath of innocent citizens."

"Maybe the citizens are willing to die for change," Jez interjected.

Miriam nodded her agreement. "Candace should take a stand. At least let everyone know she isn't murdering the Depraved. Make being queer legal."

"No! Don't you see? Then the other side, the ones who hate us, will fight back, and we'll have a full civil war on our hands."

"Maybe that's what we need," Abel said, surprising everyone. He shrugged as everyone stared at him. "Let's not pretend this isn't where the Holy USA has been heading for decades."

Everyone started talking at once. It was hard to gauge who was of what opinion, so Miriam laid into Asher. "You can't be serious. The people are letting themselves be heard. This is the time."

"Millions of people could die, Miriam." He ran his hand through his hair and sighed. His exasperation enraged Miriam.

"Some things are worth dying for! Freedom, for one." She shook her head. "You are so afraid of change."

"I'm afraid of genocide!"

"Newsflash! Genocide has already happened in this country.

People think it's still happening because you keep Candace from doing the right thing."

"I don't keep Candace from doing anything! You don't understand how precarious her control is."

"STOP IT!"

Everyone silenced as Candace, who had never sounded like more of a ruler, screamed at them. She took a deep breath, then continued. "I informed all of you because it's the right thing. You need to know what's happening. But I am the fucking queen, and I will decide what to do." She threw her hands up. "The justices are demanding intervention and are threatening to take things into their own hands. I will make a statement tonight."

"What will you say?" Miriam asked.

Candace shrugged. "I have a meeting with Reuben Alderman in an hour. I'll know more then. Miriam, Asher, if you two could stop fighting, I need your help."

18

Miriam followed Candace down a long corridor she'd never seen before. Asher was right behind her. Her feelings toward him were conflicted. She cared for him, wanted him, but his outburst at the riots was disheartening. He'd given her a longing look on their way out of the harem, and she'd just given him a sad smile in return.

"Why do you need us?" Miriam asked. She wasn't sure what Candace could need her for. Asher made sense. He'd been advising her for years. But massive riots, possibly the start of a revolution, didn't seem to call for a Domme.

"Because I trust the two of you more than anyone on my payroll."

"We're not on your payroll," Miriam retorted.

"Exactly." Candace took a right turn at a massive painting of Jesus clad in the American flag. Miriam crinkled her nose in disgust before following the queen.

"Why do you need him?" Asher asked. He'd been quiet up till now.

"Because I still have a reputation to keep, no matter what I decide."

"Him? Him who?" Miriam was curious. Seriously, where were they going? She didn't even know the palace was this big.

"I don't know what getting him involved will accomplish." Asher sounded skeptical.

Candace turned her head to look at him. "We have to, Asher. And I need your help."

"Uh, can someone loop me in? Who are we talking about?"

Candace stopped in front of a door, and Miriam nearly tripped trying to stop herself. Asher came up behind her and put his hand on the small of her back. She sighed and leaned in to his touch a little before remembering she was mad at him. And that no one was answering her question.

"I want a simple statement, Asher. Nothing that commits one way or another. And he's got to be ready for the camera in an hour. I meet with Alderman soon, so I need the two of you to take point on this."

"Hello? Take point on what?" Miriam threw her hands up. "Will one of you please tell me what is going on?"

Asher gave her a half-smile, an apologetic one. "It's time for you to meet Jonathan."

"Jonathan? As in Jonathan Sanders? The Prime Minister for God? The Sacred Pastor?" He was the highest religious authority in the Holy USA. He hadn't been as public in recent years, save for his streamed Sunday worship services. And Miriam had no idea he lived in the palace.

Candace snorted. "Sacred. Ha."

The queen banged on the door, and they waited for several minutes in silence. No one came to the door.

"Jesus Christ," Asher muttered under his breath. Then, louder, he asked Candace, "Do you have it?"

Candace shook a small vial. Then she pressed a button on the door to activate the retinal scanner, peered into the device, and stepped back when the door slid open.

Miriam coughed as a pungent odor of alcohol, weed, and some other horrible smell seeped into the hallway.

"Apologies in advance," Candace said before stepping into the smoke filled room.

The curtains were drawn, and only one lamp in the corner was on, casting a low light in a large bedroom. Miriam blinked as she adjusted to the low light. Clothes and papers were strewn across the floor, and Miriam couldn't help but imagine the bedrooms of the teenager boys she'd sneaked out of in high school. In one corner, a large bed held three naked bodies, the blankets barely covering them.

"Wake up Jonathan!" Candace yelled. She turned toward Miriam with a grimace. "Sorry, he's hard to wake up."

"It's the drugs," Asher said.

Oh, that's what that other smell was. Miriam recognized the scent of Burning Bush, a designer drug she'd only encountered in clubs. It really fucked a person up, so she had always avoided it.

This was not the preacher she was expecting.

"Wake up!" Candace shouted again. This time, one of the women in the bed sat up and blinked at them with confusion. She was nude, her slight frame bony and her face gaunt. She jostled Jonathan's shoulder until he stirred.

"Someone's here," she said in a stage whisper.

The other woman sat up. She had stringy blonde hair and dark circles under her eyes. "That's not just anyone. That's the queen."

Jonathan groaned but didn't move. "What do you want?" His voice, so polished and smooth on camera, was thick with drugs and sleep.

"Get up, asshole. We have a situation." Candace folded her arms. Clearly, this was not the first time she'd found him in such a state. Asher stood, a look of exasperation on his face. Miriam just gaped.

Jonathan turned in the bed to face them, his penis on full, flaccid display, but he made no move to get up. "What's going on?"

"Take this first. I don't want to repeat myself." She handed him the bottle. Jonathan pulled himself into a sitting position with an exaggerated groan, took the bottle, unscrewed the cap, and snorted whatever was inside. The bloodshot in his eyes cleared in an instant. He sat up straighter and rolled his shoulders back. He turned his head from side to side, cracking his neck, and when he spoke, he was no longer thick-tongued. Miriam's eyes widened at the sudden change.

"Now, what is so important that you need to interrupt my time with these beautiful ladies?" He turned his head to look at the women and blanched. "Anyway, it's not Sunday, is it?"

Candace filled him in. Miriam stepped closer to Asher and whispered, "What the hell did she give him?"

"SoberUp."

"Damn. Rich people have all the cool stuff. I could have used that a time or two."

Asher raised a brow. "You've partaken in Burning Bush?"

"Fuck no." Miriam shook her head emphatically. "Nope, just drank myself into oblivion a few times. Had a hell of a hangover."

"I did it once in college. Never again." He shivered. "Listen, Miriam, about earlier... I don't want to fight."

Miriam folded her arms, drawing herself inward. "I guess that depends on a few things."

Asher swallowed, his Adam's apple bobbing. "You're right that things need to change. That people should have the right to rise up. It's just...I don't know. I feel responsible, and I don't want more people to die."

"You're not responsible, Asher." Miriam cocked her head. "Why would you think that?"

"Because I advise *her*." He jerked a thumb toward Candace. "And she *is* responsible."

"You're not the queen, Asher."

He pressed his lips together in a firm line. "But... Forget it. I know I'm a coward, okay? But I don't want to lose you because of it."

Miriam was stunned. She reached out and took his hand because she didn't know what to say. She had no idea he felt responsible for the entire fucking country, and she frankly thought it was ridiculous.

"What happened to you?" she whispered low enough that she wasn't sure if he heard. He just squeezed her hand.

Candace turned around with a look of surprise on her face. "Well. Glad to see you two got your shit together."

"Why does everyone keep saying that?" Asher wondered aloud.

Candace laughed. "You're the smartest person I know, and also the dumbest." She flipped her hair behind her shoulder. "Now, I only have a few minutes. Get him to the set and work on what he'll say."

Jonathan reached down from the bed and grabbed a pair of dingy boxers off the ground. "Asher, are you going to introduce me to your new...whatever?"

"After you put real clothes on, Jonathan." He wrinkled his nose. "Are those even clean?"

"Clean enough." Jonathan slid on his boxers, then looked at Miriam with a charming grin. "I'm Jonathan."

"I know. Everyone knows who you are." She noticed the slightest slip of his smile, but he recovered quickly, a well-practiced facade on his face. "I'm Miriam."

"Ah. New resident of the queen's beloved harem?"

Miriam raised her chin, surprised he knew about their existence. This was the man who extolled the sins of the flesh, after all. But then she had found him drugged-up and in bed with two women that she was starting to think were prostitutes.

The longer she lived in the palace, the less everything made sense.

Jonathan disappeared into the bathroom, leaving Asher and Miriam alone with the women. Asher cleared his throat. "Has he paid you yet?" They both nodded. Definitely prostitutes. "Good. Please leave." The women scrambled out of the bed to collect their clothes, and Miriam and Asher turned around to give them a bit of privacy.

Miriam could tell it wasn't the first time Asher had dismissed prostitutes on Jonathan's behalf. This whole day was beyond bizarre. She'd woken up in bed with Asher, found out her disappearance had started riots, and now learned the most holy man in the country was a hedonist.

Her head ached.

The women left, and a few minutes later, Jonathan emerged from the bathroom, freshly shaven and showered. He was dressed in a fine suit of electric blue, a white bamboo turtleneck underneath. There'd been some controversy, Miriam recalled, when he first took on the title and had shunned the ties of his predecessor.

"Too casual to preach the word of God," she remembered people saying, yet he looked anything but casual.

The fashion in the Holy USA was decades behind the rest of the world, with their sustainable, breathable fabrics more focused on comfort than design. But even Miriam had to admit he looked sharp. Like an authority. And definitely not a man who was drugged out of his mind a few minutes ago.

"You have a Moses Tablet I could borrow?" Asher asked him. Jonathan pulled a sleek glass screen off his desk.

"Ridiculous that she doesn't let you have your own," Jonathan said. Miriam had to agree, but Candace didn't want the harem residents accessing their old accounts and letting people know they were alive. She could just restrict their access, but Miriam had hacked more than her fair share of tablets, so she supposed Candace had a point.

Asher tapped away on the screen. She leaned over to see what he was doing. "Are you writing a prayer?"

"Yes. Ironic, isn't it? The atheist writing the prayer for the preacher?"

"He doesn't write his own?"

Jonathan laughed. "I'm more than capable. But for these political things"—he waved a hand—"Candace prefers Asher to write them."

"These riots aren't just some political thing," Miriam retorted. "People are fed up. They're ready for change."

Jonathan studied her, and Miriam found his green stare unnerving. Assessing. "A bleeding heart, huh?" A slow smile crept over his face. "My dear, you'll soon find that everything is political. Even you."

19

The world was on fire, and Asher had never been happier. His nagging guilt hadn't left, of course. It was just part of who he was at this point. Perhaps that was his curse—after all his hard work helping Candace keep relative peace in the country, he could only be happy once that peace was destroyed.

It had been a week since the first riots broke out. The police forces had squashed some of the smaller riots, but Memphis, Dallas, and Manhattan raged on, growing in number by the hour. They'd breached armories, and they were only killing in self-defense. Barricades in neighborhoods held more than just a threat of violence. Food banks, medic tents, song and prayer circles had popped up in every barricade, according to Candace's intelligence. Depraved living their authentic selves inside the protection of the protests. The footage was inspiring, and Miriam was smug about it.

"See? Have some faith in the people," she'd said.

But there were counter-protests, too, though they were smaller. People who just wanted to kill the Depraved or anyone different would attack barricades in broad daylight. At night, the police showed up, trying to bring down the bases, but they rarely got close enough. Brave people and stolen drones defended the encampments, the sound of bullets drowned by the sound of singing and chanting.

Maybe Miriam had been right all along.

Miriam. He wanted to spend every waking moment with her, wanted to worship her body until his dropped from exhaustion. He did the best he could. Unfortunately, they now comprised Candace's advisory council. And the queen needed more scenes than normal from her Domme to cope with the turmoil. But every night when Miriam returned to the Residence, he took her in his arms and made love to her until they were both too tired. Mornings came earlier, and they lived on generated coffee and carbs.

Miriam thrived in her advisory role, impressing Asher. She asked questions no one else considered when they received daily intelligence debriefs. She mined appropriate Bible verses for Jonathan's now daily prayers. Asher felt more than a little useless, but he could make Miriam come and scream his name. Maybe that was his purpose all along. When she was with him, the flashbacks about his sister were minimal. Yes, the world was on fire and Asher felt the most normal he had in eight years.

Right now, he lay in Miriam's bed with his arms behind his head. Miriam sat next to him, knees up and arms around her legs. "I just think it's odd that there's no manifesto or list of demands yet."

"Why? Do you think they're organized enough for that?"

She turned her head and arched an eyebrow at him. He'd asked a stupid question. All the intelligence suggested some greater organization. How else had they set up the barricades so quickly? Asher put his arms out in surrender. "You're right."

"My favorite words," she teased. Then she let out a huge yawn, and Asher frowned.

"You're overworking yourself," he said.

"Maybe you're overworking me," she said as she yawned again.

He smirked, but he felt a twinge of shame. He should let her rest, but every night he ached for her. Miriam was keeping his demons away for now, plus she was so damn delectable. Addictive.

"Tell Candace you can't see her tonight."

Miriam shrugged. "She needs the release. Plus, isn't that my entire purpose of being here? I could be scrubbing palace toilets."

"There are robots for that." He pulled himself into a sitting position. "She has an entire harem of people she could call on for release."

"True." Miriam stretched out next to him and leaned against his side. He wrapped an arm around her and kissed her temple. "How long until debrief?"

"A little over an hour."

She snuggled further into the bed, pulling Asher down with her. "Maybe we can just nap until then." She was asleep in seconds, and Asher chuckled to himself.

He couldn't sleep, though. Instead, his mind raced through their latest actions. At his urging, Candace had shut down media coverage of the riots on the state-run internet, but too many people had access to the uncensored internet. Soon, people outside the rioting cities would demand answers. Miriam had fought him hard on that advice, believing that honest media coverage was their best course of action. Asher thought they needed to control the narrative for now, and Candace agreed.

Healthcare justice Levi Pierce had shut down hospitals near the barricades almost immediately. Candace had reamed him a new one, according to Jonathan, now sober for a full week and attending meetings with the queen. There were innocent people, including children, in those hospitals who had nothing to do with the protests. But Pierce didn't care.

Noah Westcott over Agriculture was also threatening to shut down supermarkets, but everyone knew he was too greedy and didn't care where his profits came from. He also generally allied with Candace.

Reuben Alderman was still a wildcard. He hadn't questioned Candace when she told him to leave the cops to handle the riots, but he had sent additional weapons to the police forces. Asher was quite sure they'd paid a pretty penny for it and Alderman hadn't acted out of the goodness of his heart. Or badness, depending whose side you were on.

Candace still hadn't made a public statement. She was relying on Jonathan to be the face people saw, but Asher knew it wouldn't fly for long. Once more coverage reached banned social media sites, people would start demanding answers from their queen.

He sighed. He had no more answers than he did yesterday or the day before. Candace was listening to him less and less, and he couldn't help but feel a little resentful. He'd advised her for years. But then a voice echoed that he hadn't done his job well after all. If he had, these blood-filled protests wouldn't happen. Doubt and shame crept into his throat, and he squeezed his eyes closed. Did he break everything he touched? Everyone he loved?

He glanced down at Miriam. If he wasn't careful, he could slip into a blinding love and end up hurting her, too. If something happened to her, he'd never forgive himself. And he couldn't carry any more on his conscience. It was full.

He had to protect his conscience, protect her from *him*. But when she curled around him in her sleep, his heart constricted with conflicting emotions. Asher hadn't had a nightmare about Bethany since he'd started sleeping with Miriam.

But weren't those nightmares and flashbacks his absolution? Didn't he deserve them?

He didn't trust himself not to hurt her. But he wasn't sure he trusted himself to pull away, either. Asher was a weak man, and even his best attempts at making amends for his choices had failed. He wasn't strong enough to resist his attraction to Miriam, and he didn't want to.

Yes, the world was on fire, and as usual, Asher had only himself to blame.

20

M iriam felt like a horrible Dominant when she asked Candace for the night off, but Asher had been right. She was exhausted. Her arms ached from leading impact play, and her brain never stopped thinking about the riots, even when she was in a scene with Candace. The queen was a constant reminder of what was happening. The only time the thoughts stopped swirling was in bed with Asher. Or the shower. Or the pool, although they'd gotten their asses chewed out by Jez for that one. Come to think of it, Jez was chewing everyone out.

Candace had been gracious, though, and even apologized for overworking Miriam. Miriam shrugged off the apologies. She had big plans to curl up with a fantasy novel in the library, and she hoped Asher would join her. He was comfortable to be around in silence, and he loved to read even more than she did.

The intelligence briefing had been short that day, with no real new information. The only news was that the footage had leaked into other countries, and they were condemning the lack of leadership. Candace just took the news with a stone face, still unwilling to address the people. It wasn't clear how much of the Holy USA was aware of what was going on. Miriam wanted to know why they *didn't* know that, and Candace had told the intelligence team to get a better read of the blacklisted internet sites.

Dressed in bamboo leggings and a sports bra, Miriam entered the library, picked up the book she'd left on the table a week ago, and curled up in the oversized armchair. She'd been reading for five minutes when someone cleared their throat.

Miriam glanced up to find Esther standing in the doorway, an apologetic smile on her face. "Hey, Miriam. Can I talk to you?"

Miriam stifled a sigh. She wanted to be left alone, but quiet and demure Esther had never asked her for anything. "Sure. What's up?"

Esther shuffled further into the library but made no move to sit down. Miriam sat down her book and tried to put an inviting expression on her face as she waited for Esther to speak.

"So, last week...the party." Esther's cheeks turned red. "You did a great job getting that together."

"Uh, thanks." Miriam leaned back in her chair and folded her arms. "Don't be shy, Esther. We all had an orgy. I think we're past any awkwardness."

Esther let out a giggle. "True." Her face turned downward, she mumbled, "I want you to teach me."

Miriam's eyes widened. Esther was so docile, so timid most of the time. She knew that Esther had been to a BDSM club once before her arrest, but she hadn't pegged her for a Dominant. And she was normally so great at figuring out people's kinks and desires. "Teach you to be a Domme?"

Esther nodded, her face even redder. "I've always wanted to learn. I've just never felt confident. And...well, now is a good time to learn."

"Why now?"

Esther's chin dipped. "It's stupid."

"Come on, Esther. If you want to apprentice with me, I need to know why you want to learn." Patting the seat next to her, Miriam smiled. "Whatever you say here stays here."

Esther approached the seat and perched on the edge as if she were afraid to get too comfortable. "Something happened between Elijah and me that night."

"You slept together?"

Esther scoffed. "Well, we tried. But Elijah has some needs that I just couldn't meet."

Miriam understood. "He's very submissive."

"Possibly the most submissive I've ever heard of," Esther agreed. "It started out fine, and then I just couldn't be what he needed me to be." She chewed on her lower lip.

Understanding dawned on Miriam. "You have feelings for him."

"Yes."

"Have you talked to him about that night?"

Esther shook her head. "I think we're both too embarrassed."

"Well, the first thing you need to do is talk to him. If you want to learn to be more dominant, you need to feel comfortable having these conversations."

Esther glanced up with a hopeful expression. "You'll teach me then?"

"I'll teach you, but your first assignment is to talk to Elijah, no matter how awkward it is. Then you can start watching me with Candace tomorrow night."

With a huge grin, Esther jumped up and threw her arms around Miriam. "Thank you! Thank you so much!"

"Are you going to tell Elijah that you're going to learn how to top?" Miriam asked.

Esther shrugged. "I need to get a feel for what he wants. He may not reciprocate at all." She cringed. "It was so awkward, Miriam."

"Sometimes sex is awkward. That's okay." Miriam smiled. "I think you and Elijah could be great together, for what it's worth."

"Thanks, Miriam." Esther turned and left the library, so Miriam picked her book back up. Not two minutes later, Asher knocked on the doorframe. She glanced up and grinned.

"Hey! You want to join me for some reading?"

Asher shook his head. "I wish. But she's summoned us."

"Fuck. It must be important."

The two of them headed to the elevator that led to Candace's apartment. Asher made no move of affection toward Miriam, which struck her as odd. He'd been so affectionate, but now he seemed aloof. He was probably just worried about whatever Candace had to say. Hopefully.

The elevator dinged, and the doors slid open to reveal Candace pacing her living room. Her hands shook, and her normally pristine hair looked mussed, as if she had run her hands through it repeatedly.

"Candace?" Miriam asked in a low voice.

"What's wrong?" Asher stepped into the apartment first, and Miriam stood a step behind him.

Candace kept pacing as she said, "It's bad. It's really bad."

"What? More riots? Is it Alderman?" Miriam stepped forward and put a hand on Candace to steady her.

Candace blinked. "Much worse."

"What is it, Candace?" Asher sounded exasperated. "Spit it out."

The queen pointed to a small piece of paper on the coffee table. Asher reached forward and grabbed it. "Fuck."

Miriam yanked the paper from his hand and read, *I know your secret. I know about the harem.*

"Fuck," Miriam echoed. "Who is this from?"

Candace shrugged. "I have no idea. It was laying on my pillow when I came up for a nap." She ran her hands through her hair. "This is bad. This is really bad."

Asher furrowed his brow. "Do you think it's one of the justices?"

"I don't know."

Miriam sat down on the pink sofa and folded her arms. "How would a justice get this up here? I thought everyone in the palace was loyal to you."

"Anyone can be bribed, Miriam." Asher's voice was condescending, and Miriam arched an eyebrow at him, resisting the urge to flip him off. "Have you checked the records to see who accessed your room?"

"Of course I have," Candace snapped. "I'm not an idiot, Asher. Not even housekeeping has been up here today."

"So it was someone who erased the evidence," Miriam said.

"Clearly." Candace sighed. "But who? And how do they know?"

Asher finally sat down in the chair across from Miriam. He spread his long legs out and crossed his ankles, a pose Miriam had recognized as his thinking pose. "You don't think Jonathan told anyone?"

Candace shrugged. "I don't think so."

"Then someone is leaking information from the palace."

Miriam's brow furrowed. "I don't understand why this is so

bad. You're the queen. You're entitled to do whatever the fuck you want inside your palace."

"If this gets out to the public, it would be catastrophic," Asher replied.

"How so?"

"Everyone would realize that she's been lying. She's one of the very Depraved that are illegal in this country." Miriam opened her mouth to speak, but Asher cut her off. "Don't say she should just change the law. At least half of the Supreme Court would turn on her. Candace and all of us would be in danger."

"At least half the Supreme Court is already against her."

"And let's not forget what life was like before she took over all the arrests. It would be like that, but worse. Cops attacking anyone they thought was queer, only this time with no faith in their leader."

"Or she could enforce a new law since, you know, she is the queen."

"Could you two stop bickering? And stop talking about me while I'm right here?" Candace threw her hands up. "Asher is right, Miriam. If news of the harem gets out, the justices could usurp. I know some of them have been looking for a way to do it for years."

"Then defend your throne. You're not weak."

Candace's shoulders slumped. "I'm so tired. A new protest broke out in Chicago. News is leaking, despite our best attempts to filter it." She held up her hand to Miriam. "Don't say anything. We have to control the narrative."

Miriam sat back. They didn't have to control the narrative. She didn't understand why Candace wouldn't just exert her power. Either shut down the protests or speak on them or do literally anything. And Asher wasn't helping things. For whatever reason, he felt it was his job to keep peace in the entire country. But what neither of them understood was that peace hadn't existed in a long, long time. Rapes, kidnappings, murders, burglaries were rampant in the cities. Cops didn't care. Once, Miriam knew there had been entire units of detectives for cases like that. But justice didn't exist anymore.

Not to mention the control the justices had over society and the instability that caused. Families that couldn't afford privatized education sent their kids to work as young as ten. Any teen who teachers found suspicious were hauled off to conversion camps—and that trauma would live with Miriam forever. Hospitals refused to treat the poor. Rents went up at random intervals, Housing evicted people at random, and food was getting more and more expensive.

The country was unstable. Just because cops weren't murdering the Depraved anymore, thanks to Candace, didn't mean peace existed.

"Candace, you have to address the public," Asher said, breaking the silence. Finally, he said something that Miriam agreed with.

"And say what?"

Asher went silent again. Miriam thought about her conversation with him earlier, and how there was no list of demands or manifesto. Maybe they thought no one was listening.

"Speak directly to the protestors," Miriam suggested. "Tell them you're listening. Ask them what they want."

Leaning forward with his elbows on his knees, Asher nodded. "That might just work. A show of good faith that you're taking them seriously."

Candace sighed. "That's going to piss a bunch of people off."

"That's kind of in your job description," Miriam replied.

"It's not a solution," Candace said. "And admitting that there are riots we can't control isn't a good look."

"Silence isn't either." Miriam gave Candace a small smile. "You've been silent for far too long, Candace." She didn't just mean since the protests started, either. Whenever Candace spoke, she gave speeches of nothingness. Platitudes and patriotism. Just like Jonathan's sermons and prayers.

But the two of them were the most powerful people in the country, no matter what the justices controlled. It was time for them to start acting like it.

21

C andace tasked Asher with the unfortunate task of telling everyone in the harem they could no longer leave the Residence and wander the palace unless they had strict instructions from the queen herself. Everyone raged, and not even telling them that someone knew about their existence worked. Jez went on a curse-filled tirade before slamming off to their room. But no one was more upset than Marah and Abel, who lived for palace gossip. Asher had a feeling he'd be hearing about this nonstop for weeks.

Miriam had left to go take a nap, which left Asher alone to work on Candace's speech. The plan was for her to go live the following day. She'd already had her media team announce the broadcast before Asher had left her apartment. Then she'd gone to find Jonathan and assign him to write a prayer for after her speech.

After a couple of hours, Asher stretched his hands. He wished he could type on a tablet, but if only he was allowed access to the technology, everyone would riot. He still didn't understand why they couldn't have locked-down personal Moses Tablets besides the ones for music and movies in their rooms, but Candace worked hard to keep everyone a secret.

And somehow, she had failed.

He squeezed the bridge of his nose. Part of him wanted to blame Abel and Marah for their gossiping. They were hardly ever in the Residence during the day; instead, they spent most of their time with friends and frenemies in the greater part of the palace. Could they be responsible for leaking the information to someone outside the palace?

No, they knew what was at stake: their lives. That meant someone on staff had leaked the information. And for what? Their own existence was at stake, too. If anyone found out that Candace staffed her homes with all the Depraved she was supposed to execute, it would be a disaster. Right now, only the ten residents of her harem were in danger.

He cracked his knuckles. Maybe he should follow Miriam's lead and take a nap. But he had avoided sleeping in his room since he and Miriam had started sleeping together. Beth's pictures adorned his walls, and he didn't want to think about her right now.

Fuck, he was a terrible brother. He was avoiding his sister's memory, and for what? A chance to fuck someone after years of celibacy? He was weak.

Weak and cowardly. Miriam had raised so many great points in the last week, he was almost convinced she was right. Maybe it was time for Candace to come forward and make some changes. But with Alderman's allegiance unknown, the risk of not having Defense on their side was too big. He was terrified of another Great Ablution, a genocide with millions dead for some supposed sin.

"Hey." Miriam's soft voice jolted him out of his thoughts.

He looked up at her. God, she was beautiful, with her sleepy eyes and mussed-up hair. "Hey."

"Can we talk?"

He gestured at the seat across the small table. "Sure."

She sat down and leaned forward on her elbows. "How's the speech coming?"

"Good, I think." He shrugged. "Can you take a look at it later?"

"Sure." She smiled. "Thanks for backing me up about this."

Asher's stomach swirled with guilt. He hadn't backed her up at all, except for agreeing that a speech was a good idea. He said nothing, instead opting for a nod.

"Are you mad at me?"

"About what happened upstairs?"

She shook her head. "About anything. You seem off."

"I'm not mad at you, Miriam. Just have a lot on my mind." He reached across the table to take her hands in his. Gestures like this would not help him keep his emotional distance, but he couldn't seem to help himself. Miriam was soft and warm and good. She was a balm to his soul, and God knew his soul needed a respite.

"I don't like feeling like we're on opposite sides, Asher." She squeezed his hands. "It makes things complicated between us."

He sighed. "I don't like it either. We're both stubborn. For what it's worth, I do see your side of things. But we don't know the loyalty of the Department of Defense. We can't risk a civil war."

"I'm afraid it's inevitable."

"I know." They sat there in silence for several minutes, just holding each other's hands. Asher broke the silence first. "It doesn't have to complicate sex, Miriam. My opinions are nothing personal."

A flash of some emotion he couldn't read crossed her face, but it was gone in an instant. "Right. Sex." She rolled her shoulders back and let go of his hands.

Shit. What did he say wrong? "I don't want to fight with you, Miriam. Can we agree that when we're here, we are on the same side?"

She gave him a smile that didn't quite reach her eyes. "Of course."

"Come here." He scooted his chair back and patted his lap. "I don't know what I said, but let me make it up to you."

She hesitated before standing up, but she came to him. She sat down on his lap, her legs perpendicular to his. Wrapping his arms around her waist, he pulled her close and whispered, "You're so beautiful."

This time, her smile was real. He brushed her hair aside and nibbled her earlobe. Within minutes, she was squirming and squeezing her legs together. Blood rushed to Asher's cock, the feel of her lush ass doing no favors for his erection.

"Let me make you come," he whispered in her ear. She mewled.

He slipped his hand inside her leggings to find that she wasn't wearing any underwear. All the better, he thought. His fingers played in the thick curls of hair on her mons.

"Stop fucking teasing me, Asher, and touch my clit."

He yanked on her hair, making her gasp. He bit the side of her neck as punishment for her sass.

"More," she breathed.

"Bratty little switch." He chuckled against her neck before sinking his teeth into the sensitive spot where it met her shoulder. Meanwhile, his fingers inched lower and found her slick with want for him. He grazed a fingertip over her clit, and she rolled her hips.

"Mm. Naughty girl. I should bring you all the way to the brink and not let you come."

Miriam stiffened. "I don't like edging." She turned to face him. "We should probably do some negotiations if we're going to continue this."

Asher flushed with embarrassment. "You're right. I'm sorry."

"But later." She kissed him and licked her tongue across his lips. "For now, go back to playing with me."

"Yes, ma'am."

"Now, that's more like it."

Asher laughed. "We can't both be dominant here."

"I don't know. I think we've been doing a pretty good job." She slid her hand over his and began to guide him to stroking her. He set a steady pace, and she relaxed in his arms. Her long, dark hair fell behind her, and he curled his fist into it.

"I love your hair." He leaned forward and breathed in the scent of coconut from her shampoo. Half the harem used the same shampoo, but only on Miriam was it so arousing.

"I love your talented fucking fingers," she replied, panting.

Asher's lips crashed onto hers, pulling her closer to him by the hair. It was a searing kiss, an apology for disagreeing with her, for continuing to disagree. An apology for whatever he'd said that had upset her a few minutes before. It was an apology for just being him, for breaking everything he touched. He begged with his kiss to not be turned away, to not be let go.

She opened her mouth and invited his tongue in. He swiped his tongue against hers, then sucked on her lower lip. His fingers continued to explore her core. He had two inside her and his thumb fondling her swollen, wet clit. She wrapped her arms around his neck to kiss him deeper, and her hips pushed against his hand. He could come like this, he thought, like a teen coming in his pants.

But she didn't let him. Her orgasm came quickly. She clenched around his fingers, and her arousal coated his hand. She went still, letting out a quiet, "oh!" against his lips.

With one hard pat to her swollen clit, causing her to groan, he slipped his hand from her pants and licked his fingers clean. She tasted salty and sweet, a taste uniquely hers, and he couldn't get enough. "Let me eat you out," he growled into her ear.

"Not right now. I have something else in mind."

She slid off his lap and onto her knees. Asher threw his head back as she pulled the fabric of his pants over his swollen, aching cock. He spread his legs to give her better access to him, and she leaned in and licked the beaded moisture off the tip. Her wet, velvet tongue swirled around the purplish head.

She licked up from the base to the top in slow, torturous strokes. Asher tensed, trying not to come just yet. He wanted to savor every minute of this. Miriam didn't get on her knees for just anyone, and her mouth was so damn talented. With a quick wink, she took him into her mouth and slid him in as far as he could go.

She swallowed, which created an intense sucking sensation, and Asher nearly levitated off the chair. She chuckled with a mouthful of his cock, sending vibrations deep into his belly. Moaning, she sucked him even deeper until he hit the back of her throat.

"Jesus fucking Christ, you're good at that."

She met his eyes with her own hazel orbs, looking beyond

erotic. She bobbed her head in a slow rhythm, enough to drive him wild but not make him come. After a few moments, she popped off with a smack. Asher's cock glistened with her saliva.

"I want you to fuck my mouth," she murmured.

Asher groaned. Then he stood, wrapped one hand in her hair as she knelt, and used the other to guide his cock to her wet, swollen lips. "Open up that gorgeous fucking mouth, darling."

She obeyed, and her submission sent a heady rush to Asher's brain. The significance of this wasn't lost on him, and he was sure later she'd take back her power. But she was offering him vulnerability, and it tasted almost as delicious as she did.

"Fuck," he said as he glided over the flat of her tongue.

Slowly, he began to thrust into her mouth, giving her time to adjust. He wound both hands in her hair and kept her head locked close to his groin. Her hands ran up his thighs and onto his buttocks, where her nails dug in as she pulled him even closer. He let out a sound between a laugh and a pant. She was still in control, and she wanted more.

He fucked her mouth harder, without warning. She took him like the good girl she was, working through every gag, every time he hit the back of her throat. Tears streamed down her face, and as soon as he was about to check in with her, she moved one of her hands and slid it down the front of her pants.

His hips snapped harder now, and he was close. His balls tightened. As if she knew, she took her other hand and began to fondle them, squeezing lightly. One thrust. Two. Three. And he was spilling down her throat. She took everything he gave her.

He pulled his sated cock free of her mouth. She wiped her spit-and-cum-soaked mouth with the back of her hand but made no move to wipe the tears from her cheeks. Asher tucked himself back into his pants, then sat back down. He cupped her beautiful face with his hands and wiped her cheeks with his thumbs. She sighed a contented sigh.

That sigh that let Asher know he was well and truly fucked. He could try to keep his heart guarded, but it would do no good. No good whatsoever.

He was falling in love with Miriam. Or maybe he had already.

22

The next day, the queen summoned Asher on his own before the intelligence debrief and her address. He placed a quick kiss on Miriam's lips, then headed up to Candace's office, the floor below her apartment.

Candace sat at her desk, bathed in sunlight from the wall of windows behind her. Asher hated this office. It was overly pink, like everything else in Candace's part of the palace, and he often felt like he needed sunglasses just to talk with her.

"Any news on the leak?" he asked as he took a seat across from his oldest friend. "Or who sent the note?"

She shook her head. "I have intelligence looking into it."

"Good. If someone is leaking information from the palace, we need to know. I noticed you ramped up security." More armored robots lined the hallway between the Residence and the elevator, along with two additional guards. He hoped they were people they could trust.

"Yes." She leaned forward and put her elbows on the desk, steepling her fingers in front of her. "I've added more security to the perimeter as well. But that's not why I called you up here early."

"What's up, Candy?" He didn't know what could be so important or secretive that she didn't call Miriam or Jonathan up, too.

She slid a Moses Tablet across the desk, and Asher took it. On it were two people he didn't recognize. They were older than middle-aged. The woman had brown hair and full cheeks. The man had black hair tinged with gray. "Who are they?"

"Intelligence got close enough to the leaders in Memphis to get photos. These are two of the main instigators."

"Well, that's good news, I guess."

Candace frowned. "No, this is bad news. We've identified them, of course." Every citizen's face was in the national security database, so finding out their identities wouldn't be hard.

He hated when she didn't get to the point. "Who are they, Candy?"

"Those are Miriam's parents."

"What?!" Miriam had given no inkling that her parents would be involved in something like this. Her mother was a schoolteacher, and her father had a government job at the Department of Technology. Had they always been rebels or was this because of Miriam's disappearance?

"It gets worse."

"How could it get worse? She's going to be so upset."

"Her father is dead."

Asher blinked. "You told me intelligence just got these photos."

Candace slumped forward and buried her head in her hands. "I know. Then he went out on the front lines last night. He didn't make it back."

"Oh, Candace." Asher was in shock. "Miriam is going to be so upset."

"If I tell her."

Asher stared at Candace. "What do you mean *if* you tell her? Why wouldn't you?"

"Because I don't know how she'll react! What if she tries to contact her mother?"

She would be well within her rights to try, Asher thought. Although without access to an unlocked tablet, he wasn't sure how she would. Still, Miriam was smart.

"What if she wants to leave, Asher?"

He drew in a sharp breath. That thought hadn't occurred to him. But what if she did? Where could she even go? She no longer existed according to the national system. The only option Candace ever gave to leave was to try their luck in the DMZ. But what if she fled in the night? Tried to go to her mother?

"You have to tell her, Candace. She deserves to know."

Candace slumped in her chair. "But I can't do this without her. She's become invaluable. And, frankly, I don't want her to leave."

"I don't either." His heart ached at the thought of losing her. Shit, he was in over his head. "But Candace, if you don't tell Miriam, she will find out. And you know she deserves the truth."

"Tell me what?"

Fuck. Neither of them had heard the door open. Candace's eyes were wide. Slowly, Asher turned around to see Miriam and Jonathan standing in the doorway. Miriam's hands were on her hips as she looked at them expectantly.

"Tell me what?" she repeated.

"Miriam..." Asher began. But she held up a hand to stop him.

"It sounds like Candace has something to tell me." Her voice had a sharp edge to it. "Tell me, Candace."

Candace inhaled. "Sit down, please." She gestured at the chair next to Asher. Miriam plopped down and folded her arms. Asher reached over to put a hand on her leg, but she shook him off.

"I have some terrible news, I'm afraid." Candace was trembling, and Asher realized that she had fallen for Miriam, too. "It seems that your parents were some of the leaders of the Memphis protests."

"What? Are you sure?" Miriam dropped her arms to her sides and leaned forward. "That can't be right. My parents are the most apolitical, boring people."

"We're sure. We received their photos from intelligence yesterday."

"And you're sure they're leaders?"

Candace nodded. "They were."

"This makes no sense." Miriam pressed her fingers to her temples. "Wait, what do you mean 'they were' leaders?"

Candace looked to Asher, her face twisted in pain. Asher sighed and took Miriam's hand. "Your father. He was killed last night. On the front lines."

Miriam's lip quivered. "F-front lines? You're wrong. He's just an engineer. He's not a soldier. He's not..." She looked at Asher's face and whatever she saw there broke her. Asher moved his chair closer and pulled her against him as sobs racked her body.

"Miriam, I'm so sorry," Jonathan said in a low voice. Asher had all but forgotten the preacher was there.

"Me, too," said the queen.

Miriam raised her head up. She glared at Jonathan,

then settled her stony gaze on Candace. "Fuck you. You're responsible for this. Both of you are."

Jonathan's shoulders slumped forward. Candace sat back in her chair and waited for whatever Miriam had to say.

"The suffering in this damn country is your fault. These people have hit a breaking point. You—" she pointed her finger at Jonathan "—feed them lies every Sunday about God choosing this country and sin and the gospel of wealth that you preach." She turned back to Candace. "And you. You have ignored the suffering for your entire reign. You refuse to stand up and be a leader."

Miriam threw her hands up. "How many other parents of missing Depraved, or accused Depraved, are out there protesting? How many more dead citizens will it take for you to understand that their blood is on your hands?"

"Miriam..." Asher said, but she held out a hand in response.

"No. You have encouraged this blindness to the plight of our people." She stood abruptly, knocking Asher back a few inches in his chair. "All of you are responsible for this. You're responsible for the deaths of my parents and so many others."

Candace's lower lip quivered, though she tried to remain impassive. Asher could see the strain on her face. The worst part was Miriam was right. They'd spent so long playing it safe that they'd ignored the suffering. More was at stake than the safety of the Depraved. Most of the citizens were suffering in some way—they had no freedom.

Once, America had touted freedom as its mantra, but that time was long past. Christianity, an illusion of safety, a belief that a theocratic rule had the best interest of God and man...they'd made enemies of most of the world, who had moved toward a more equitable democracy. Shut off from the world at large, America had become an island of devastation and desperation.

Miriam stormed out of the room, shaking in anger, her face wet with tears. After a few minutes of stunned silence, Jonathan left, too, without a word, leaving Asher once again alone with Candace.

He turned toward his old friend, the queen. With her face contorted, she looked as if she'd aged ten years.

"She's right, you know," Candace whispered.

"I know." He rubbed his face. A dull ache settled in his stomach. Miriam's words haunted him—he'd spent so long trying to be good, to make amends for his sins, to keep his people safe. But in doing so, he'd kept Candace from being the ruler she needed to be. "I'm sorry, Candace."

The queen shook her blonde head. "For what, Asher? This is my country. I've been willfully ignorant, too hellbent on keeping the peace with the justices." Her face softened. "This isn't on you."

But Asher didn't believe her. She'd put her trust in him as her adviser. He held just as much blame, if not more.

"I have to make a stand," Candace declared.

Asher rubbed his face with his hand. She was right, but the thought was terrifying. "What will you do?"

Candace shrugged. "I'm not sure yet. But it starts with asserting my power over the Supreme Court. They don't make the laws in this country."

"They control so much of our society, though. It's risky."

"Yes. But they aren't doing anything to help the citizens, anyway. And we have Gideon Thorne and Noah Westcott on our side." The justices over Technology and Agriculture had always supported Candace, had never acted against her.

"Will they remain on your side if you suddenly change a bunch of laws?"

"I hope so. Westcott will, I think. He can't cut off everyone's food supply and shut all the supermarkets. He likes his money too much."

"What about Kingsley?" Asher asked. Solomon Kingsley controlled the entire energy industry. He'd always been a wildcard. Sometimes, he defended Candace, while other times he pushed back. But unlike most of the justices, he seemed to have a bit of a heart. He'd installed more solar and wind farms after his father had died, decreasing the country's dependence on oil. The rest of the world had all moved toward clean energy decades before, but Kingsley's predecessors had claimed oil was the way of God.

Candace placed her hands in front of her. "I don't know, Asher. I really don't."

"You should meet with them privately. Feel them out, let them know things are going to change."

"I'll arrange that as soon as possible." Leaning forward, she fixed her gaze on Asher's eyes. "Now, about Miriam."

He sighed and waited for her to continue. What was there to say? He was worried about her, but after her lashing out, he doubted she wanted to see him.

"Ash, you've given me tons of advice over the years. Now it's time for me to give you some." She leaned back and folded her arms. "Don't fuck this up."

"What?"

"You heard me. Don't fuck up what you have with Miriam.

You've been punishing yourself for nearly a decade. But it's time for you to move on. Miriam is special, and she's obviously in love with you."

Asher gaped. "No, she's not. You heard what she said."

"She was hurting."

"It's just sex, Candace." Even as he said it, he heard the lie. Candace arched an eyebrow at him. "Fine. What do you propose I do?"

"Find her. Comfort her. You're the smartest man I know. I'm sure you can figure it out."

He squeezed the bridge of his nose. "Candy, I'm scared that this is over now."

"Don't let it be." She sat up straight, looking more royal than Asher had seen her in a long time. "Now, you're dismissed."

23

Miriam paced the rooftop garden, unable to escape the urge to run. There was nowhere to run here, save a treadmill downstairs. The harem had never felt like more of a prison than it did now. Her mind swirled with grief and disbelief and confusion. What the hell were her parents doing in these protests? *Her* parents. Her boring, sweet, never-political parents.

They'd never so much as uttered a word of disagreement—or agreement, come to think of it—with the monarchy in her entire life. They talked about work and the weather and the price of eggs. When the school had shipped Miriam off to conversion camp for being too outspoken (and therefore potentially Depraved), all they'd said was that they loved her.

Had they always been tapped into rebellion, or was it just Miriam's disappearance? A wave of nausea hit her. If she was responsible for her father's death...she was, wasn't she? If Miriam hadn't been Lady Lilith, hadn't frequented queer sex clubs, hadn't made herself an enemy of the state, would her father still be alive? And how long until her mother was next?

Miriam peered over the edge of the roof toward the east. Memphis wasn't far from the capital. If she could just get past the palace security, maybe she could make it. Then she could find the barricade, find her mother, convince her to go home.

Or she could ask Candace to have her mother apprehended. Bringing her to the palace would keep her safe. Miriam could see her, and they could grieve the loss of her father together. Candace would do it, Miriam was certain. Of course, now her mother was more of an enemy of the state than Miriam had ever been. Maybe Candace would just throw her in prison, but at least then she'd be safe.

Fuck. There was no good solution. Miriam couldn't take that choice from her mother. Her own future, her own choices, had been taken from her by Candace. Her mother believed in what she was fighting for. Still, if there were some way to let her mother know she was alive.

Miriam took a deep breath. The scent of pine from the mountains and flowers from the garden filled her nose, grounding her just the slightest bit. She blinked as the crisp breeze stung her eyes. Fall was just around the corner. Soon, she'd learned in school, the trees would begin to change colors to red and gold. She'd never seen it before in the concrete jungle of the city.

A memory of her father popped into her mind. He'd grown up on a farm until he was twelve, when his parents shipped him off to the city for school. He was the brightest of his siblings, and they'd saved for years to send him to a better education. But he'd seen the seasons change, had even glimpsed blue skies untainted by smog. Miriam recalled his stories and his desire to take her to visit the farm one day. When his parents died, that dream died, too. Getting days off from the Department of Technology was impossible, and he'd been unable to attend the funerals.

She turned her face to the sun. The sky was almost blue here, outside of the capital. She let the sun beat down on her face as tears streamed from her eyes. Her parents deserved so much better. Deserved a better daughter, one who called home more than once a month. One who hadn't committed treason.

Unsure what hurt worse, the guilt or the grief, she folded her hands across her aching stomach. Her breaths came in short, shallow pants as the sobbing recommenced.

"Miriam?" a quiet tenor asked from behind her. She squeezed her eyes shut, trying to stop the tears from falling. Wiping her face, she turned to see Asher standing a few feet away, his face full of concern.

She opened her mouth to speak, to greet him, to say anything, but no words came. He held out his arms, and despite herself, she stepped into his embrace. A loud howl of despair escaped her, and he tightened his arms around her. He kissed the top of her head as she soaked his shirt with her cries. She hated herself for showing her weakness, but his chest was the rock-solid foundation she needed as her soul quivered with the instability of grief.

Unsure how long they stood there, Miriam hiccupped as her sobs became whimpers. For the first time since he'd embraced her, she could hear the thumping of his heart in his chest. She tried to take a few deep breaths as she let the percussion steady her.

"What do you need?" he whispered into her ear. "What can I do?" His voice was helpless.

"Just this." She sniffled into his shirt. "Just this is enough."

With a quick squeeze, he released her, sat down, and tugged her onto his lap. She curled against him. "Tell me about your parents."

It was the right thing to say. She purged memories of her parents onto his listening ears. How her father would lift her up on his shoulders for parades on national holidays. How her mother gently taught her to read before she ever started school. She talked about using the pool at the facility for government employees, how her dad had taught her to swim. She recalled helping her mother grade assignments while her mother cooked and cleaned. They worked long hours, and Miriam had spent much of her childhood in daycare or school or alone at home. But the moments they had shared had been good.

She never knew hunger until she branched out on her own. She'd been too proud to ask her parents for help, but they would have aided her in a heartbeat. They'd attended her college graduation, each taking a precious sick day to support her. They were hard workers, patient and kind.

"I just can't wrap my head around it," Miriam finished. "They never gave me any inkling that they had any opinions of the government whatsoever. I'm just scared that…"

Asher nuzzled his face against her hair. "Scared of what?"

"Scared that his death is all my fault. And what that means about me."

"That you're selfish? Reckless? Twisted deep in your soul?"

She raised her head to look in his eyes, her own stare surprised. "Yes."

He gave her a small smile. "You're none of those things, Miriam. You sacrificed your own safety for the safety of thousands of others. You avoided being caught for years." He placed a gentle kiss on her lips. "And most importantly, you're good. You care like no one else I've ever met."

"But if this is all because of me, because they think I'm

dead—"

"Then it's pride that led them to rebellion, Miriam. If they were ashamed of you, do you think your mother would be out there right now in the barricade? That your father would have sacrificed his life on the front lines if he was even the slightest bit embarrassed of you?"

Miriam wailed. Though she hadn't thought she could cry anymore, tears fell again. Asher hugged her as she rode out the wave of emotion.

They were quiet a long time after the tears stopped. She breathed in his scent of sandalwood soap. She was spent from crying so much, and all she wanted to do was sleep. But Asher's words played over in her mind.

"You know how I felt because that's how you feel." He stiffened. "Asher, you're *good*. You're not twisted. And I don't think you are selfish or reckless."

He inhaled sharply. "I was, though. Beyond selfish and reckless."

"What happened to your sister, Asher? Will you tell me?"

He hung his head, avoiding eye contact. "I'm too scared of what you'll think of me."

"I don't think..." She shook her head. "I know your heart, Asher."

"One day, Miriam. I promise one day I'll tell you. But not today." He leaned forward and kissed her shoulder. "You don't need to hear it today."

He was right. She couldn't handle any other emotions today, but she also didn't know how she could think less of him. Whatever he'd done, surely it wasn't that bad. He hadn't murdered his sister, but for whatever reason, he held himself responsible for her death. Miriam had spent hours trying to guess the story, to no avail. She knew it involved Candace and had something to do with Asher being queer or kinky. Those were her only clues.

Another day, then. For now, she just wanted to sleep. She kissed Asher, a gentle, chaste kiss, then gathered herself from his lap and stood. "I'm going to take a nap," she said.

He smiled sadly. "Do you want me to join you?"

"No, I think I want to be alone right now."

"Okay. I'll be around if you need me."

With a final glance, Miriam left Asher alone in the garden and went downstairs to collapse into bed.

24

After a few minutes alone on the roof, Asher descended the stairs back to the harem. He glanced at a book in the library, but he didn't feel like reading. He made his way down the hallway and stood in front of his bedroom pod.

He'd been avoiding his room since he started sleeping with Miriam, only going in long enough to change clothes. His room was a shrine to his sister. Bethany's pictures lined the walls, hung with reverence so he'd never forget her. He couldn't avoid her any longer.

He sat on his bed and stared at the pictures. Bethany laughing. Little Bethany with her brown hair in pigtails. Adult Bethany trying her first sip of alcohol, a hilarious grimace on her face.

"I'm so sorry, Beth."

He'd said the words thousands of times, and thousands of times they'd fallen flat. Sorry wasn't enough. It would never be enough. The image of her limp body flashed through his mind, and he felt as if he were choking. Better that image than what had come before, he thought grimly.

But memories of what had happened to Beth hadn't plagued him in well over a week. Miriam was a balm for his tormented mind, and the guilt crashed into him. He had broken his punishment of chastity, and he hadn't dreamed of Bethany once. But he was also avoiding the memories, avoiding his own stupid bedroom so he wouldn't have to look at his sister.

Coward.

He smacked his hand into his forehead once, twice, three times. Fucking coward. That was the theme of his life. It's what Miriam had all but said earlier in Candace's office. His cowardice hadn't kept people safe. Instead, it had led to a full rebellion, what he'd wanted to avoid at all costs.

And now he couldn't even look at pictures of his baby sister because what? It would mess up his ability to have sex. Selfish. Still so selfish. In the eight years since her death, he hadn't learned anything.

A knock sounded at his door. He wiped his eyes.

"Come in," he said, his voice command activating the lock.

The door slid open. Elijah stood with a grin on his face, which turned into a furrowed brow. "Asher. What's wrong? Is it Miriam?"

Asher let out a dry laugh. "Yes. No. I don't know."

"What's going on?" He stepped into the room and sat down on the bed next to Asher.

He didn't even know what he wanted to tell Elijah. Even his best friend didn't know all the details of what had happened to Bethany. Only Candace knew because she was there. He cleared his throat and started with the safer topic. "Miriam's father died in the rebellion in Memphis."

"Oh my god."

"Yeah, turns out her parents are...were...some of the organizers."

"Does she know?"

Asher nodded. "Yeah. She's asleep right now."

Elijah took a long look at Asher, long enough that Asher squirmed. "Are you somehow blaming yourself?"

His friend was too intuitive. "Shouldn't I? This rebellion directly results from Candace's inaction, which I've been advising her on for years."

"Asher, you and Candace have done what you thought was right."

"But it wasn't right!" Asher jumped up and threw his hands in the air. "We've ignored so much. I've encouraged Candace to be a doormat for the justices. I was wrong, Elijah. And now we have rebellions breaking out in every major city. How many people are going to die?"

Elijah shrugged. "Those people are out there because they want to be. Need to be. This was inevitable, Asher."

Asher wasn't so sure. He knew their country wasn't perfect, but since Candace had been crowned, state-led violence had significantly decreased. Or so he'd thought. Hearing Miriam talk about life in the slums told a different story.

"You believe that?"

Elijah nodded emphatically. "I really do, Asher. People can only tolerate a dictatorship or an oligarchy or whatever the fuck this mess of a country is for so long. It's illegal to be yourself. Police kill whenever they feel like it. Prices are exorbitant because of those bastards on the Supreme Court. People are starving and angry."

Asher pressed his hands against his eyes. "So, what's the outcome? All I can see are tens of thousands of people dying against nine private militaries."

"Yeah. I don't know, Ash. I'm glad I'm not sitting in on these meetings like you and Miriam. But something has to change. Something *will* change. It's past time."

"What if they fail?" He raised his head to meet Elijah's eyes.

Elijah gave him a half-smile. "Don't let them." He paused, then waved his hand. "Now, scoot over and tell me everything about you and Miriam."

"You've slept with her, too." It came out far more accusatory than Asher meant for it to. He tried to cover it up with a small smile.

"And out of respect for you, I won't anymore. But I'm not talking about the sex."

Asher groaned and flopped backward on the bed. Elijah reclined next to him and folded his arms behind his head. "You used to tell me everything, you know."

Memories of growing up together entered Asher's mind. Working on school projects, playing pranks on Beth and Elijah's little sister Abigail. The pubescent experiments in Elijah's massive bedroom. Asher chuckled a little, which caused Elijah to give him the side-eye.

"Just reminiscing." He ran a hand through his hair. "It's nothing personal. You know that, right?"

"I know. But I worry about you. I've worried about you for years."

When Beth had died, Elijah had rushed home from filming. He was one of the few people who knew it was suicide—too many undertakers would have refused service, even to Asher's affluent family. Elijah had been there for Asher, but instead of letting him in, Asher withdrew further and further into himself. And now, years later, he was only starting to suspect that maybe his penance hadn't been quite right.

"I'm okay."

"I think you're starting to be okay. Because of her."

A lump formed in Asher's throat. He coughed, but his voice still came out hoarse. "Yeah. Maybe."

Elijah sat up. "Asher. Don't fuck up a good thing. You deserve this. You deserve happiness. Beth wouldn't want you to be miserable forever."

We don't know what Beth would have wanted, Asher thought, but he kept the words inside. Elijah was just trying to help. And he was right—Asher ran the risk of letting his own issues get in the way of whatever he had with Miriam. The problem was, he still wasn't sure he deserved it, deserved *her*.

"I'm trying, Elijah. That's all I can do." Elijah was trying, too, and Asher knew his friend deserved better. Maybe things would never be like they were before, but it was worth a shot. Elijah had been nothing but good to him. "So, what's new with you? I saw you disappear with Esther after the dungeon party."

His friend groaned. "I don't know, man. I like her, but..." He trailed off. "Sometimes I think there's something wrong with me."

"What do you mean?"

Elijah hedged. "It was just awkward. So, I have no idea what's going on."

"I'm sorry."

"Yeah. Me, too." Elijah pasted a movie star smile on his face. "Come on, brother. Let's go smoke a joint, then play some pool or something."

A genuine grin spread across Asher's face. "You've never had a better idea. Lead the way."

25

"Are you sure you're up for this, Miriam?" Esther asked as she tied her brunette hair into a ponytail. "Maybe I could ask Asher to help me."

A streak of jealousy ran through Miriam at that suggestion. That was a new sensation. Miriam had long believed she wasn't a jealous person, but the thought of Asher doing anything with Candace or Esther or anyone made her feel nauseated. Besides, Asher wouldn't step into his dominant nature, even to train Esther. It came out some in bed with Miriam, but whatever his deep, dark secret was keeping him from being his authentic self. Frankly, Miriam was getting a little fed up with the brooding martyrdom.

She pressed the generate button on Candace's wardrobe MolecuMaker. The machine whirred to life as it began forming a latex bodysuit. "I'm fine, Esther."

"We could wait a few more days."

"No." Miriam was tired of grieving. Crying had wrung out Miriam's body. Asher had been great, but he'd treated her like a porcelain doll. She was ready to get some normalcy back. Not that living in a harem as the queen's personal Dominatrix was *normal*, but a routine was nice. And she had more than a little anger to take out on Candace, who would eat it up like dessert.

Not quite as satisfying when the person you were angry at liked it, but it would have to do.

Miriam grabbed the completed bodysuit and looked at Esther. "All right, strip down."

Esther made a face. "I'm not sure I can pull that off." She gestured at her body.

"This is going to fit you like a glove."

"That's what I'm worried about."

"Esther, you are luscious and absolutely perfect. Now get to stripping, woman."

Esther gave her a small smile, but uncertainty still danced in her eyes. Still, she took off her flowy paisley dress. "Are you sure the latex is necessary?"

"Necessary? No. But you lack confidence. You've said yourself you've fantasized about dominating all the time. That makes me know you can do this. You need confidence, though, or you can't sell it, and nothing makes you feel more confident than fetish wear."

It took a few minutes of grunting and pulling, but soon Esther was dressed in bright red latex with a zipper up the torso. Miriam tugged the zipper down to show off more cleavage before positioning Esther in front of the three-way mirror. "Look at you."

Esther beamed at her reflection. She moved her hands over the swell of her breasts and the fullness of her hips. "I look good."

"Damn right, you do. Don't forget it again." Miriam adjusted her corset and smoothed down her hair. She handed Esther a tube of scarlet lip gloss. "Final touch."

Lips applied, they made their way to Candace's bedroom.

Esther had a bounce in her step, and Miriam knew she'd done the right thing. Candace was kneeling by the bed as they entered her massive suite. She glanced up, and a grin spread across her face.

"Well, well, well. Look at you," she said in a husky voice.

"She didn't give you permission to speak," Miriam replied in a stern voice. Oh, it would be hard to keep the anger at bay tonight. She inhaled and looked at Esther. "Make sure they know who is in charge. They have the power to safe-out. They set the boundaries about what happens to their bodies. But don't let them forget you are the one in control."

Esther followed Miriam to the wardrobe where all the goodies waited. Miriam opened the doors and began naming some items and what sensation they would achieve on their intended victim. Miriam watched as Esther's eyes twinkled. Her hands ran over the various implements of pain and pleasure. Finally, she settled her grip on a leather riding crop. She glanced at Miriam for approval, and Miriam grinned. "Excellent choice."

An hour later, Miriam left Esther in charge of Candace's aftercare. She yawned as the facial recognition device on the robot solider recognized her. The door to the harem slid open. It was midnight, and she was looking forward to crashing in her bed, perhaps cuddled up next to Asher, who was sitting on one of the low sofas in the main room with a book in his hands. A warm smile spread across Miriam's face. It scared her a little, how much Asher was feeling like her sanctuary, but tonight, she just craved his presence.

"Hey," he said. He closed the book and set it aside. "How'd it go?"

Miriam draped herself across the sofa and put her head in his lap, and he stroked her hair in smooth, firm motions. She practically purred. "Esther's a natural Domme."

"Really? I'm a little surprised."

"I'm not. I've seen a lot of the quiet ones have a natural dominant streak." She closed her eyes and enjoyed the feeling of Asher's hands in her hair. "What were you up to tonight?"

"Poker."

"Did you win?" She looked up to see him smirk.

"I didn't do half bad. But Isaac won."

His hands trailed from her hair to her neck and clavicle. She moaned and arched into his touch, forcing his touch onto the tops of her breasts. "I want you tonight."

"Are you sure you're ready?" he asked, his voice full of concern.

Miriam huffed. "I will not stop having sex just because my dad died, Asher."

Asher stiffened. It was the wrong thing to say; after all, Asher had all but become a monk when his sister died. Miriam didn't understand it, but she hadn't meant to be so harsh. His journey was his own. With the mood sufficiently killed, Miriam changed the subject.

"Tell me about her." She sat up and curled her legs underneath her so she could see Asher better. He leaned his head against the back of the sofa and sighed. For a while, Miriam didn't think he was going to answer. A couple of minutes passed before he spoke.

"She was hilarious. Just had the best timing for a quip. No one could make me laugh like she could. I think that might be what I miss the most." For the first time, Asher relayed several stories about Bethany. His body eased the longer he talked, his hands getting more and more animated. Miriam chuckled, savoring this vulnerability from the man she was falling in love with. Maybe, just maybe, there was hope that he could heal his demons.

Miriam's laughed turned into a yawn, and she glanced up at the large tablet screen on the wall. It was nearly 2 a.m. Asher grabbed her hand and squeezed. "Come on. Let's go to bed."

He stood and pulled Miriam to her feet. She wobbled a little, and another yawn escaped. "Okay. But in the morning, we're having sex."

Smiling, he planted a quick kiss on her lips. "You're insatiable."

"And you love me for it," she said groggily. Asher said nothing.

26

Despite the media being state-run, word of the riots spread like wildfire over the next few days. More rebellions began in more major cities. Candace had relented on her media-ban for the harem residents, and they now spent hours watching illicit footage from the front lines. Cries of "Stop killing our children" and "Stop starving us" haunted their ears. Every time Miriam closed her eyes, she saw the police in riot gear beating peaceful protestors, who held only signs to defend themselves. They'd all but stopped arresting the rebels as the prisons were bursting at the seams.

Miriam finally attended the daily debriefs with Candace, Jonathan, and Asher again. But when she entered Candace's office a week after her father's death, she found a camera crew setting up in front of the queen's desk. A makeup artist was busy powdering Candace's face in one corner. Jonathan and Asher stood in another corner in front of a white background, heads bent low as they discussed something.

"What's going on?" Miriam asked.

Candace's face lit up, and she waved the makeup artist away. "Good! You're here. I was hoping you would come. I'm addressing the country about the rebellions again."

"Finally," Jonathan muttered.

Candace rolled her eyes. "Yes, it's about time. But we've been working on what to do and say. I'll speak, then Jonathan will do a sermon."

"What are you going to say?" Miriam plopped down on the rose-colored sofa.

Before Candace could answer, one of the camera crew interrupted. "You're on in two minutes, Your Majesty."

The queen swept her blonde hair over her shoulders and took a seat behind her desk. The heat from the light equipment was stifling, and Miriam wasn't sure how Candace managed to sit in front of the blazing lights without sweating. Asher came and sat next to Miriam while Jonathan remained standing in the corner, holding a well-worn Bible. It was the only hard copy of a Bible Miriam had ever seen.

"Quiet on set," the person Miriam determined must be the director said. She held up her fingers and counted down from five. Candace transformed into the authority she was right before their eyes. She commanded respect, and even Miriam couldn't help but feel it.

She began with a smile. "My fellow Americans, by now you have likely heard—or witnessed firsthand—the riots in our cities. I would like to first apologize for the palace's reticence on the matter."

An apology? This was new. Miriam leaned forward.

"We had hoped that these rebellions would disperse in a few days on their own. Instead, they have spread. This speaks to a deep and troubling sense of discontent among you, the people. I have been monitoring these movements closely, and I have come to several conclusions. With the guidance of Reverend Jonathan Sanders and my closest advisors, along with many hours spent in prayer, I've determined that it is time to make some changes."

Miriam's heart pounded, but she tried to keep her optimism at bay.

Candace continued, "I have been in talks with Justice Westcott. We hear your pleas about the cost of food, and you can expect to see a dramatic drop in prices at your local supermarket. The last thing we want is for anyone to go hungry."

It was too late for that, Miriam thought, but she appreciated the gesture. Maybe it really would get better for at least some Americans.

"Reverend Sanders and I have been discussing theology at length. Citizens, this monarchy made a mistake decades ago. We all know the Great Ablution of seventy years ago was the deadliest event in our nation's long history, followed closely by the Second Great Ablution." She paused. Her chest rose and fell as she took a deep breath. "We were wrong. We used verses in the Bible to advance a policy of genocide."

Miriam blinked. This couldn't be happening.

"I'll allow your sacred minister to give you the Biblical evidence in a few minutes. But I want you to hear it from me first. It is not a sin to love people of the same gender as yourself. The more I learn about Christ, the more I see a message of love. I'm tired of the hate. Effective immediately, it is no longer illegal to be one of the Depraved. Anyone seeking to harm one of these individuals will be subject to the full power of the law."

Candace's placid face faltered for the briefest of moments. She seemed to weigh her next words. "This issue is dear to my heart. I've struggled with shame and confusion long enough. As your leader, it is my role to lead this country to greatness, and I can no longer, in good conscience, condone the arrest, abuse, and murder of my own community."

Miriam turned to Asher, mouth agape. He smiled at her; he'd known what was coming then. But Miriam couldn't believe it. Candace had just come out on a national broadcast. She had the strangest urge to rush behind the desk and kiss the queen square on the mouth, though she refrained.

"I know many of you will have questions, and I will do my best to answer them over the coming weeks," Candace said. "For now, I will allow Reverend Sanders to give us all spiritual guidance to navigate these changes. God bless you all."

Candace waited until the director gave Jonathan the signal to start speaking before collapsing forward on her desk. Miriam got up and tiptoed over to the desk, then wrapped her arms around the queen. "Thank you," she whispered. Candace's silent tears wet Miriam's shirt.

Jonathan's sermon was his best ever, and he'd written it himself. He cited the handful of verses condemning homosexuality, pointing out that Christ said nothing about it. He discussed translations and the way the Bible had changed over millennia, and he did so in easy-to-understand terms. Impressed, Miriam realized Jonathan had been in his own sort of prison. He was intelligent and a powerful orator, and he'd been chained to a narrative he didn't believe in. Candace, too, had spent her life bound to a role that she didn't fit. Although she'd been held back by fear, she had the makings of an amazing leader. Whatever came next, Miriam believed Candace could handle it.

The sermon lasted for about twenty minutes. After, the camera crew packed up, leaving Miriam, Asher, Candace, and Jonathan alone in the royal office.

"You did it, Candy," Asher said. He stood to hug his old friend.

Candace heaved a sigh and squeezed Asher tight. "I did it."

"How does it feel?" Miriam asked.

"Honestly? Terrifying. I have no idea what to expect."

Jonathan looked grim. "I think we can expect backlash."

Everyone nodded in agreement. This would not be some miraculous fix to all the problems. Too much deep-seated hatred and bigotry ran through the people of the country, especially the people in power. And Candace had all but guaranteed that the Supreme Court would split.

Miriam chewed her lip. Would this at least end the riots? Would it result in witch hunts against the queer citizens? "What now?"

Candace shrugged. "Now, we wait."

27

The violence grew with each passing day. The queen had made new enemies with her decree, and now each city had two factions: the initial rebels and the vigilantes who sought to destroy them. Whose side the police were on depended on the city. Candace dispatched military forces to take over and keep the peace where possible, and she increased security at the palace. On the rooftop, once a refuge for the harem residents, they could hear gunfire and bombs in the distance at the fringes of the capital.

Candace was a blubbering mess most of the time. Her enemies in the Supreme Court harassed her and threatened her. She found another note, this time on her desk, that read, *You made a dangerous choice.* She shut down access to her room to everyone but her harem and her most trusted guard, who was now in charge of supervising the people who cleaned her rooms.

Asher couldn't shake the feeling that they'd made things worse. It had only been four days since Candace's address, and they still didn't know what the Supreme Court would do. Thankfully, Solomon Kingsley, Energy Justice, had thanked Candace and declared his loyalty. The only wild card that remained was Reuben Alderman. They needed his support because his military was the largest and his technology the strongest. If he turned against Candace, Asher feared the monarchy would fall. They were all in danger.

At least things with Miriam were going well. Together, they channeled their anxiety about the state of the country into explosive orgasms. He talked more openly about his family, including Bethany. For the first time since his sister died, he felt like maybe he might be whole again.

Just in time for a civil war.

It was nearly time for the daily debriefing with intelligence. As Asher and Miriam dressed after their morning romp, shouts sounded from downstairs. Asher raised an eyebrow at Miriam, who shrugged.

"That sounds like Jez," he said.

Together, they made their way downstairs. Candace and Jez were in a standoff, standing in the center of the main room. The rest of the harem stood on the outskirts, taking in the scene.

"It's out of the question!" Candace yelled. "I won't allow it!"

"You did this, you bitch!"

Asher and Miriam stopped next to Marah. "What's going on?" Asher whispered.

"Jez wants to leave," Marah said in a low voice. "They want to go fight."

Tears streamed down Candace's face. "Jez! You'll die!"

"That's my choice. You can't make that decision for me."

"I can, and I will!"

Back and forth, they sparred. Jez raised some good points. Since Candace had lifted the ban on queerness, how could she keep everyone she'd saved that lived in her various residences? But Candace had points in her favor as well. It was dangerous.

Jez no longer had a chip—they effectively did not exist anymore. They wouldn't be able to even purchase a bottle of water without a chip.

"Surely you can get me a new one, if that's what you're so worried about," Jez said.

Candace rubbed her face. "You're not letting this go, are you?"

"No, Candace. I *need* to be out there."

The queen plopped down on a sofa and crossed her legs. She looked around at her audience. "What about the rest of you?"

No one said anything. The air was thick with tension. Even Abel had nothing to say for once.

Asher broke the silence. "Can I suggest something?"

Everyone turned to look at him. Jez's face was bright red, and they looked like they might attack anyone who came near them. Candace looked at Asher expectantly. He folded his arms across his chest, unsure how they would receive his idea.

"Could you work with intelligence, Jez?"

Candace cocked her head, thinking. "That's a great idea."

Jez was silent for a few minutes. Finally, they said, "If it gets me out of here and onto the front lines, I'll do it."

Wiping away tears, Candace said, "I just don't want anything to happen to you, Jez. I care about you. I care about all of you."

For the first time since their fight started, Jez softened. "I know. But this has to be my choice."

"You can always come back."

Somehow, Asher knew Jez wouldn't. If they survived, and he hoped they would, they would stay gone forever. Of all the harem residents, Jez was the most unsatisfied with their luxurious prison. And he couldn't help but wonder who would follow in their footsteps. He looked around. Some twiddled their thumbs while others studied the floor. He loved these people. They'd become his family, and a flash of regret passed over him. He'd never opened up the way the others had.

Miriam grabbed his arm and leaned her head against his shoulder. He glanced down to see her eyes brimming with unshed tears. He leaned down and kissed the top of her head. "They'll be all right." He believed it, too. Jez was smart and strong. Plus, intelligence would hook them up with some tech. They could always call for help. "Jez is a badass. The rebellion needs them."

"Yeah." She sniffled.

"Fine then," Candace said, her voice thick with emotion. "Come on, Jez. Let's go meet the intelligence team." She stood and held out her hand to Jez in a peace offering. Jez took it with a small smile.

"Thank you."

Asher gestured for Miriam to go ahead, and they followed Jez up to Candace's office. They paused as the added retinal scanner scanned Candace's eyes. It was an upgrade from the facial recognition software. As he crossed the threshold of the office door, Asher couldn't help the premonition that the harem was falling apart. Who would be the next to leave?

28

Asher's tongue could sing hymns between Miriam's thighs for eternity. He pinned her hips down with his strong hands as she writhed beneath his ministrations. Her little mewls of pleasure jolted straight to his cock; he'd already come once this morning, but he was weak to her passionate noises. And God, did she make noise in bed. If there was a heaven, he decided, it had to include Miriam's pussy.

She was close. Just before she came, he slid his tongue away from her clit, down her slit, to her rear entrance. He swirled his tongue on the sensitive flesh there as she bucked against his face.

"Fuck! Asher!"

He smirked. It was a nice stroke to his ego that he hadn't forgotten how to fuck in his years of celibacy. Of course, he and Miriam had practiced enough over the last few weeks to gain back any lost skills.

Her body quaked as her orgasm ripped through her. He placed a kiss on her inner thigh as her shaking softened. She hadn't said anything else about love since her sleepy comment a few nights before, but in this moment, he thought that losing himself to loving her was possible. He just needed to let go and let her in.

He crawled over her, laid beside her, and folded her into his arms. She nuzzled into his chest. "Let's just stay in bed today."

"Mm. That's tempting," he said. He sniffed her hair and smelled strawberries. "Did you switch shampoos?"

"I stole it from Candace's shower."

"Great. Now she's going to need security in her bathroom."

Miriam giggled. It was nice to inject a little levity into their situation. They had to, or they'd go crazy. Someone was trying to scare Candace. Factions had developed in the cities. So far, the violence hadn't spread to the rural areas. Candace spent hours screaming over virtual meetings with the Supreme Court. And Jez was gone. The harem felt incomplete without them.

"But really, Asher. Let's play hooky today. Does she need us for every daily briefing?"

Asher sighed. He'd been advising Candace for so long that it felt wrong not to show up. But when Miriam stretched her naked, luscious body against him, he forgot everything that mattered to him.

"Let's just come back to bed after. We can make some snacks and watch an old movie." The palace had access to all the movies before the media bans eighty years ago. Lately, they'd been watching some vintage sci-fi about superheroes called the *Marvel Cinematic Universe.*

"Ugh. Fine." Miriam sat up and rifled through her clothes drawers. "Let's get this over with."

The debrief didn't take long. There was no real news, except that Justice Pierce with Healthcare was demanding information about the rioters to ban them from his hospitals. Asher figured it wouldn't be long until no medical care was available, even at the exorbitant prices the evil justice charged. Candace refused to give him any of the identities her intelligence team had collected.

Apparently, she'd called him a bastard, too; she was getting her footing as a forceful leader, and Asher couldn't have been prouder.

Miriam left before him to shower, and Asher was on snack duty. Despite the terrible situation, he had a jaunt to his step as he made his way to the Residence's kitchen. He was even whistling an old, upbeat hymn from his childhood when he ran into Elijah in the hallway.

"Hey, man." He greeted his friend with a smile.

"Hey, Ash." Elijah gave him a sad smile and patted him on the shoulder. "You hanging in there today?"

That was odd. "Yeah, I'm fine. You know, despite the country being on fire. You good?"

Elijah cocked his head. He looked as confused as Asher felt. "I'm good. Are you sure you're okay?"

"Ye-es? Should I not be?"

His friend's brown eyes widened. "Oh. Maybe I have the date wrong. I thought today was Bethany's birthday."

Asher froze, panic tightening his throat. He rushed into the kitchen where the nearest screen displayed the date in large numbers: August 6.

Fuck. Fuck fuck fuck. Had he even bothered to look at the date today? He always looked at it because he hated feeling like he lived in a time vortex, which was easy to do in the harem. He thought back to this morning. No, he definitely glanced at the date. Which meant he forgot his own sister's birthday.

Shame swirled in his stomach. His head felt heavy, and his legs wobbled. He grabbed at the countertop to steady himself. He couldn't believe this. How had he forgotten? What was so important that he saw the date and didn't immediately think of

Beth?

Miriam. Miriam and her temptress body. He'd fallen prey to the temptations of the flesh and forgot about the most important person in his life. And for what? Just for sex. He was a horrible brother. A monster, truly. Beth would be so ashamed of him.

He banged his head against the cabinet. A soft hand settled on his back. "Hey, brother. Easy there."

"I forgot, Elijah."

"That's okay. It happens."

Asher shook his head. "No, Elijah. It doesn't. Not to me." He rubbed his forehead. Below the shame, anger crept in, heating his face with rage. He needed to run, to escape. But he couldn't escape. He was stuck here, in the harem and in the past. "I have to get out of here."

He pushed past Elijah, who called after him, and fled to the rooftop garden. The late summer heat was sweltering, and the air tasted acrid from the near-constant explosions in the capital several miles east. The fragrance of the floral blooms choked him, overwhelming his senses. At least he was alone with the rage that boiled beneath the surface.

He paced for what seemed like forever, pulling at his hair and wiping away tears. Unsure how much time passed, Miriam's soft voice jolted him from his suffering.

"There you are. Are you okay?"

He refused to look at her. "Go away, Miriam," he said, voice hoarse with emotion.

"I beg your pardon?" She sounded shocked. Confused. He had to make her understand.

Turning, he gestured between them. "This ends now."

29

He might as well have slapped her because that's how it felt. What had gone wrong? Just a couple of hours before, they were planning to spend the day naked in bed. "Asher...what's happened?" She took two steps toward him and he held out his hand to stop her.

"What's happened is that we can't do this anymore. *I* can't do this anymore." Tears had stained his face.

"Asher, you can't do this."

"Leave me alone, Miriam," he seethed.

"Is this about your sister?" She watched as his Adam's apple bobbed, but he said nothing. She took his silence as affirmation. "Tell me what happened. Please. After everything, you owe me that."

His shoulders dropped. "Today's her birthday."

Miriam blinked before understanding dawned on her. "You forgot." He nodded. "And for some reason, you blame me?"

Another nod.

"Asher, I don't understand."

He glared at her. "You distract me."

Miriam huffed and folded her arms. "So, really, you blame yourself." He turned away, and she sighed. "Don't do this, Asher. Please. What we have is so good. So special."

"Don't you understand, Miriam? You make me forget. And if I forget…Beth deserves better."

"But she's gone, Asher. You can't keep punishing yourself."

"It's all my fault, Miriam! Her death is on my hands." He held his hands out in front of him. His big brown eyes pled with her, but she refused to stop. He owed her more than this.

"Tell me what happened to her, Asher. Please. If you want to end things, you owe me the truth."

He said nothing for several long minutes. Beads of sweat rolled down Miriam's forehead and burned her eyes. A warm breeze blew her hair, still damp from the shower, into her face, and she pushed the offending strands away. Asher hadn't stormed off, which was a good sign. She waited for him to open up, praying he would give her an answer that made this all make sense.

A distant explosion sounded, but it didn't shock them anymore. With Candace's robots, drones, and human guards, they were safe here. Miriam didn't feel safe, though. She felt as if her world was crumbling beneath her. She squeezed her eyes shut as regret threatened to choke her. Letting him into her heart was a mistake. He was too broken, and he would never be hers as long as he was chained to his demons. She rubbed at the ache in her chest.

"It was…" Asher cleared his throat. "Candace and I used to be, well, more than friends."

"I know. You were her Dom."

He blew out a sigh. "Yes. And one time, the last time, we had another man with us. Candace had picked him up at a club, and we stupidly came back to her room at the palace." He rubbed a hand over his face and paused for a moment before he continued, "Her father caught us. Right as this guy and I were kissing." His breath hitched. "I don't even remember his name, and he's dead because of me."

He dropped his gaze to the ground. Miriam waited for what this had to do with his sister. After a few minutes, he went on. "Candace begged the king to spare me, even though he'd caught me in the act of Depravity. He did, but he would not let me off the hook." A sob caught in his throat, and he pressed the heels of his hands to his eyes. "He dragged Beth in and made me watch while three men…"

Asher's shoulders quaked. Miriam clapped her hand over her mouth. "Oh, Asher."

Tears flowed from his eyes. Miriam cried, too.

He gulped. "Three days later, she killed herself. I'm the one who found her."

He fell to his knees, burying his face in his hands. Stepping closer, Miriam reached out to place a hand on his shoulders, but he jerked away from her touch. "Don't," he said. "Don't touch me."

Pain seared through Miriam. "Asher, what happened is not your fault. It's the king's."

"No! I was reckless. Stupid. Depraved."

She shook her head. "Stop it. We are not Depraved. There's nothing wrong with us."

But she understood why he blamed himself, why he kept himself locked up and denied pleasure and love. Candace's father was a tyrant. A monster. Living as a queer person under his reign was terrifying. Miriam had long moved past shame for her sexual identity, but she remembered the fear. Raids on clubs. The rampant assault at conversion camps. She remembered the counselor who promised her a way out of camp. He kept his word, but she was only seventeen, for God's sake. Sobs overtook her. She wasn't sure if she was crying because of his demons or her own.

"Don't do this, Asher," she pleaded. "I need you."

"I made her a promise, Miriam. And I've broken it with you."

"You don't deserve this punishment you've inflicted on yourself. It wasn't your fault!"

His voice was flat. "It was. And I can't keep doing this. I can't risk forgetting her."

"She was your sister. You'll never forget her." Miriam wiped at her the tears and sweat that blurred her vision. "Now you're punishing me."

For the first time in several minutes, Asher lifted his head and met her eyes. "No. I'm protecting you. You deserve so much better than me."

"But I love you."

Miriam collapsed into hyperventilating sobs. She wasn't sure she'd ever cried like this, even with the news of her father. The world was in turmoil, people were dying in droves, and the one light in her life was dimming. He was snuffing out her only chance at happiness. *Their* only chance at happiness.

Asher stumbled as he got to his feet. "I'm sorry, Miriam. I just can't let myself forget her."

"But what about me?" God, she hated how pitiful she sounded. She clenched her fist as her sadness began to give way to anger at herself and at him.

He gave her a watery smile. "You're the strongest person I've ever met, Miriam. You don't need me."

With a final glance, he left her alone on the floor of the

garden. The door to the harem slammed behind him. In the distance, a bomb went off as Miriam's heart shattered into tiny slivers.

30

A sher locked himself in his bedroom pod for days, leaving only to slip into the bathroom or grab a snack. He didn't speak to anyone when he passed them. Not that anyone wanted to speak to him—news had traveled fast, and the harem residents glared at him. He couldn't blame them, either. The breakup had been so sudden, so unexpected.

He wondered how Miriam was doing.

His heart ached; no matter how much he rubbed at his chest, the pain wouldn't subside. He knew Miriam deserved better than him and his broken soul, but she'd been a balm to him. Somehow, he grieved that loss more than he grieved Bethany now, and that realization riddled him with guilt.

He was on day five of his self-imposed hermit lifestyle when someone banged on his door. He tried to ignore it, but the knocks became louder and more persistent.

"Asher! Open up! I know you're in there."

Shit. What was Candace doing up here? Who had let her into the harem and upstairs? A bunch of traitors, that's who. He wanted to wallow in peace. "Go away, Candy."

"Absolutely not. This is my palace. Open up the goddamned door."

Sighing, Asher pulled himself up from the bed and unlocked

the door. "What do you want?"

"I want to know why my closest advisor hasn't attended a single meeting for five fucking days." Candace stepped in and sniffed. "And why he hasn't showered, apparently."

Heat flooded Asher's face. Had it been five days since he showered? Maybe that explained some glares when he went to the kitchen. He took a deep breath. "Candace, I'm not sure if you know, but Miriam and I—"

"Yes, I know. Everyone knows." She shook her head. "You really fucked up, Asher."

His eyes widened at her reprimand. "Did she tell you why?"

"Of course. You forgot Beth's birthday. I still don't understand why that meant you had to give up the best thing that's ever happened to you."

Asher gaped at her. "Because I forgot the worst thing that's ever happened."

The argument sounded weak to his ears. He tried to recall how he felt a few days ago. Anger had overtaken him, and breaking up with Miriam had been his only option. In hindsight, he doubted his choice. But now Miriam knew the truth about him, about how Beth's death fell on his shoulders. She wouldn't want him now. It was too late. He didn't deserve Miriam, anyway. It was better that things ended before their hearts became even more entangled.

Candace's voice was softer when she spoke again. "I don't know how to get you to stop blaming yourself, Asher. It was Dad's fault. Not yours."

Asher shrugged, not believing her the hundredth time she'd told him this. "I still forgot her."

Candace pinched the bridge of her nose. "You're an idiot."

"I know."

"That still doesn't mean you can waste away in your room, Asher. Miriam hasn't missed a single debrief. We've got some successful intelligence from Jez." She turned her palms up in a pleading gesture. "I need you, Asher. The country is falling apart, and I need you by my side."

He swallowed against the lump in his throat. "But Miriam...I don't know how..."

Sensing his rise in emotion, Candace folded Asher into a warm embrace. "You can't stay in your room forever. At some point, you'll need to see her."

He relaxed in her arms. Candace wasn't perfect, but she'd been a friend to him for many years. She knew him better than anyone, even Elijah. He whispered, "It's going to hurt."

"Asher, you've spent so long trying to avoid feeling anything but grief. I'm not sure you even felt that anymore. You were numb before Miriam. She brought your spark back. She brought *you* back, and I've missed you for eight years."

Her words shot straight through his heart like an arrow. He had lost himself. Perhaps that was what felt so good with Miriam; he'd found himself like he'd found a long-lost friend. He didn't deserve Miriam and her fiery goodness, but maybe he deserved a chance to be himself again. Maybe it was time to finally let go of the shame and self-loathing. Briefly, he wondered if Beth would blame him for her death. Beth was so rational, so inherently pure and good. She wouldn't even recognize him anymore, and that thought hurt most of all.

Squeezing his eyes to keep tears from falling, he said, "I'll be there tomorrow."

She tightened her hug, then stepped away. "Good. I'll hold

you to it. Now go take a shower."

Half an hour later, he stepped out of the steamy bathroom, a t-shirt sticking to his damp skin. He felt more human after a long shower, like maybe he could handle the mess he'd wound up in. He paused when he saw Miriam in the hallway a few feet away, and all those thoughts vanished. His limbs felt heavy, and his shoulders slumped. He swore he could feel the remnants of his heart breaking all over again.

"Miriam," he choked out.

She folded her arms over her chest, drawing herself inward. "Hey." They stared at one another. Miriam bit her lip. "You've been avoiding me."

"I've been avoiding everyone."

"I've been worried about you."

God, he didn't deserve her. He'd broken her heart, and she was worried about him. He rubbed at his face. "I'm fine." It was a lie, and they both knew it. To her credit, Miriam didn't press him. "I'm sorry I haven't been at the meetings."

She gave him a quivery smile. "It's okay."

"No, it's not. I have responsibilities. I told Candace I'll be there tomorrow."

"Good. We need you."

The air hung thick between them as they stood there in silence. Finally, Miriam cleared her throat. "I'll, uh, see you later." She walked past him to the staircase and descended the steps with quick, hard thuds.

Asher watched her go, his heart full of longing. Loneliness crept over him. He started back toward his room when he thought better of it. Instead, he knocked on Elijah's door. His friend slid open the door and folded his arms.

"I seriously fucked up," Asher said.

Elijah stepped aside and let Asher into the room. "You think?"

31

Blood and fire. That was the daily scene playing on Candace's massive Moses Tablet. The death toll was in the thousands and creeping steadily up. There weren't even clear sides of the rebellion anymore—just violence.

The hospitals refused to admit anyone else. Nurses and doctors quit in droves and set up field hospitals. Candace's military had established safe zones for people fleeing their burning homes. Tobias Grant with Housing had begun a witch hunt—deeming people Depraved at random and turning them out of their homes. Silas Everett, Justice of Transportation, had implemented random stops and raids on the highways, which caused the riots to spread to more rural areas. The Holy United States of America was a land of fear.

Jez was in the capital, working at a field hospital. They sent updates about which supplies were hardest to find, which businesses were still open, and the general attitudes of people to the rebellions. Most people they encountered at neutral ground supported the queen's actions. Candace sent supplies with drones, although many were shot down.

Miriam's stomach churned at the latest footage from the ground. Anti-queer rebels had set a young adult on fire, and she had to look away. She doubted her own bravery; people witnessed this live, and she had the privilege of turning her head. The screams would haunt her for the rest of her life.

She encouraged Candace to force the Supreme Court in line. They were supposed to serve the monarchy, after all, but the danger of a coup increased. The Energy justice had declared his loyalty to Candace after revealing that he had a gay grandson. The only wildcard was Alderman with Defense. Without his support, Miriam, Asher, and Candace were unsure they could maintain control of the country.

Miriam could barely focus on her daily meetings with Asher there. Trying to maintain a sense of normalcy, they sat next to each other in front of the queen's desk every day, but he was too close to Miriam. His scent lit up her brain with memories of his touch. She wanted to reach out and grab him, not even for sex, just to feel his warmth again. She still didn't understand completely why he had ended things, but at least he didn't seem angry with her anymore. Now he just seemed sad. Reserved. The way he had been when Miriam had first joined the harem.

"What do you think, Miriam?" Candace asked, jolting her from her distracted thoughts.

Miriam flushed. She'd been staring at Asher and had no clue what Candace had asked. Asher avoided her gaze, but Candace looked at her with sad eyes. "I'm sorry. What was that?"

"The police have turned on us in Atlanta, and I'm not sure I have the troops to send. Should I talk to Alderman?"

"Yes, that's a good idea. You need to force his hand to stake a side."

Candace nodded. "If we don't have his military..."

The thought was too awful to consider. Candace's private military wouldn't stand a chance against the Defense

Department, especially if Alderman partnered with other justices and their mercenary forces. While Candace's enemies had yet to publicly declare their dissent, they expected it any day. In fact, Miriam wasn't sure what was taking them so long, but she supposed civil war wasn't something that happened overnight.

"How are our medical resources?" Asher asked. Miriam ached at the sound of his voice. She blinked against the burning sensation in her eyes.

Candace sighed. "We're okay for now. But if the casualties keep rising, the stockpiles will go quick. I also worry about them getting raided on their way here. Everett's troops and their raids—you just never know."

"Get them to the palace as quickly as you can," Asher said. "Use planes."

"But our stockpiles are located around the country, so we can disseminate them more quickly and easily. Are you sure that's a good idea to have them all in one place?"

"Asher's right." She dared a glance at him, and he gave her a small smile. Oh, her heart was breaking all over again. She cleared her throat. "They're in danger. Plus, you can then reassign your guards at the warehouses to other places where they'll be of more use."

"Good point." Candace rose and smoothed out her suit jacket. "I'll have everything here tomorrow. That's all for today."

"Before we go, any word about my mom?" Miriam asked. Half of her was dying for an update, while the other half wanted to remain blissfully ignorant.

But Candace shook her head. "I haven't heard anything. I'm sorry."

Miriam sniffed and rose, leaving the office and stopping in the corridor to catch her breath. She had heard nothing since her dad had died. Maybe her mom was holing up somewhere safe, but she doubted it.

"No news is probably good news," Asher said in a low voice. She glanced up and saw him leaning against the wall opposite her. His shoulders slumped, as they usually were these last few days, but he still towered over her. His deep brown eyes were full of concern.

"Maybe." Miriam shrugged.

"I'm sorry, Miriam. I wish there was something I could do to make it better."

She choked on a half-sob and threw her arms around him. He stiffened before relaxing into her embrace. His strong arms encircled her, and she leaned her head against his toned chest. For a moment, she felt safe again. Then she remembered Asher was no longer hers, and she pulled away.

"Sorry," she whispered.

He gave her a sad smile. "Don't worry about it."

Awkwardness hung between them. Miriam pressed the button on the elevator. They waited in heavy silence, which continued on the ride back to the first floor. Miriam loathed the discomfort, but she had no idea what to say. She could only hope that with time, things between them would ease. Once they were in the harem, they parted ways. Despite the near constant presence of the other residents, Miriam had never felt lonelier.

32

That night, Asher tossed and turned. Insomnia wasn't new to him, but these thoughts of Miriam were. She'd felt so good in his arms that morning, and he wondered how he'd ever let her go. He'd been an idiot. He'd acted rashly and was paying for it, which seemed to be a theme in his life. The way she'd pulled away let him know his chance of happiness was gone. His old friend self-loathing swirled in his stomach.

He glanced at the clock. Nearly six a.m. He'd barely slept, only dozing for a few minutes at a time. Maybe he'd go up to the roof and smoke a joint to relax so he could get a couple hours of sleep. He flipped on the light and rummaged in his drawer.

An alarm sounded from the screen hanging on his wall.

Startled, he looked at the screen. Candace was summoning him to her apartment. Shit. This had to be terrible news.

He threw on a shirt, gave a longing look at his cannabis, then slipped quietly into the hallway. Miriam's door opened at the same time. She yawned. Lines from her pillow were etched across her face. She wore a loose tank and boxer shorts, and Asher pushed the inappropriate thoughts from his mind. Now wasn't the time.

"You too?" he asked, careful not to speak too loudly and wake everyone else.

"Yeah," she said through another yawn. "This can't be good."

In silence, they made their way up to Candace's apartment. The lights in the hallways and elevators were blinding this early in the morning, and Asher's limbs were heavy with the lack of sleep. When they arrived, Candace, already dressed in a suit, paced the floor, Moses Tablet in hand. Screams echoed from the device, and Asher shivered.

"Candy?" he asked.

The queen spun to face them, her eyes wide with horror. "It's happening."

"What? What happened?" Miriam stepped forward and grabbed the tablet from Candace. Her hand flew over her mouth as she watched the footage. Asher peered over her shoulder.

Blood. So much blood. Hundreds of bodies lined the ground, while only a handful rushed between them, trying to stop bleeding and assessing wounds. Ashen corpses, many with their eyes opened, were scattered through the injured victims. He blinked, his heart thudding, as he realized that some bodies wore volunteer vests and medical scrubs.

He opened his mouth to ask questions, but he couldn't find the words. Miriam, ever the brave one, asked, "Where is this?"

"Manhattan," Candace said, her voice monotone. Her hands tremored. "Pierce...he..." She took a deep, steadying breath. "Pierce's mercenaries massacred the largest field hospital in the city."

"But that was a neutral ground." Asher shook as rage washed over him.

"I don't think there is neutral ground anymore, Asher." Candace collapsed on the pink sofa and buried her head in her hands. She looked small. Tired. Miriam handed the tablet to Asher and sat down next to Candace. She pulled the queen against her and stroked her long, blonde hair.

Asher stood there, helpless and angry. "What do we do?"

No one answered him. Unable to handle the screams from the tablet any longer, he switched off the device and set it on the table. He straddled a chair backwards and folded his arms over the top rung. Candace sobbed into Miriam's chest. After several long minutes, the doorbell chimed. Asher rose to answer the door. The head of palace security, Leah, stood with her arms behind her back.

"Where's Her Majesty?"

Asher stepped aside and let her in. She was a stocky, muscular redhead, her hair pulled back into a smooth ponytail. She addressed Candace, "Your Majesty, Justice Alderman is here and demands an audience."

Candace sighed and wiped away her tears. "Bring him up."

"In here?" the soldier asked.

"Yes, in here." Leah shifted her weight, clearly wanting to say something. "You can stay here if you'd like, Leah. If that will make you feel better."

"Yes, your Majesty. I'll be right back."

No one spoke while they waited for Leah to return with the head of the Defense Department. This was a turning point, and the palpable tension threatened to choke Asher. At least they'd find out what to expect from their wildcard justice.

Ruben Alderman entered the room with entirely too much swagger for the early hour. He was an attractive man, tall and broad, his dark hair peppered with gray at the temples. He wore a tailored navy suit that clung to his muscular arms, an American flag pin on the lapel. He took in the scene of Candace's apartment and the pajama-clad Asher and Miriam who stared at him.

"It's very pink in here," he said, his voice a rich baritone. He glanced back at Leah. "I suppose there's no chance I can speak with you alone."

"No," Candace said firmly. "What do you want, Alderman?"

He leaned against the wall next to the door and folded his arms. "I'm sure by now you're aware of what is happening in Manhattan." Candace just nodded. "Good. We need a plan."

Asher leaned forward. This sounded promising.

"The Supreme Court met late yesterday," Alderman continued. "We've come to an impasse."

Candace arched a queenly brow. "An impasse? It's early, Alderman. Speak plainly."

He inclined his head. "Today, the Departments of Healthcare, Education, Housing, and Transportation will be calling for your immediate departure from the throne. If you do not comply, they will seek to forcibly remove you from power."

"Took them long enough," Candace muttered. "And what of the Department of Defense?"

He deflected. "You've caused quite a stir, Your Majesty. And I have to wonder if you were too rash in legalizing Depravity." Candace said nothing, and they all waited for him to continue. "No matter. What's done is done."

The queen rubbed her temples. "Get to the fucking point. Please."

"My loyalty has always been to this country and its people. Unfortunately, those people seem to be divided. I do not, however, condone massacres of innocents. I plan to send troops out to meet Pierce's troops. We also need to increase protection at neutral grounds across the country."

Oh, thank God. Asher let out a breath he didn't know he'd been holding. Alderman glanced over and gave him an appraising look before turning back to Candace.

"And what of the attempt at a coup?" Candace asked. Asher was impressed at how she was controlling her emotions. She'd come so far from the timid woman who'd taken the throne seven years ago.

Alderman placed a hand over his heart. "You wound me, Your Majesty." Candace glared at him. Miriam looked ready to slap him. "A coup is a terrible idea. My job is promoting stability in this country, not instability."

It was a politician's answer, but for now, at least, it seemed Defense was on their side. Or at least, they didn't have to worry about his forces storming the palace.

He continued, "You have to put a stop to the rebellions. Your enemies on the Supreme Court are going to occupy all your resources."

"My resources are limited."

"Find more. Westcott over in Agriculture is sitting on a mountain of them. I'll help where I can." He brushed off his suit jacket and straightened his posture. "Wonderful talk. I'll send you my plans this afternoon for your approval."

Without a backward glance, he slipped out of the door. Leah, who'd stood in a corner, followed him to escort him out.

"What do we need to do?" Miriam asked. "What's the plan?"

Candace shrugged. "I don't know yet. I need to put out a message about the massacre before Pierce can somehow turn it against me. Guess I'll call up the broadcast team." She patted

Miriam's knee. "You two should go back to bed. We'll have a lot of work to do in the coming days."

Like Asher could sleep now. But he stood and crossed the room to where Candace perched on the sofa. He leaned down to kiss her cheek. "Alderman is an asset. This is a good thing."

"Yeah, I guess," she said. "It only took a massacre for him to declare his loyalty. And I'm still not sure he's truly on our side."

33

The traitors on the Supreme Court dispatched their mercenary forces into the cities under the guise of breaking up rebellions. Alderman had successfully disbanded many of the barricades, leading to an influx of rebels needing shelter in neutral territory. The Defense forces fought back against the rebels on the front lines while Westcott's private military defended stadiums and arenas full of displaced citizens.

Miriam spent hours poring over numbers with Asher and Candace. Casualties. Inventories of medicines and supplies. Available troops. The death toll climbed every day, and she dreaded the new reports. At least she felt like she was doing *something*. But part of her needed to do more than sit at a desk every day. Jez had left, and they were still delivering weekly reports from the capital. Maybe Candace would let Miriam do some humanitarian work at one of the shelters. She doubted it, though.

When she'd accepted the queen's offer to be her Domme and live in the harem a few months ago, she'd wanted to exert power over the queen, to make her see just how badly people suffered under her rule. She never expected to be advising her through a civil war. Candace trusted her as much as she trusted Asher now.

Asher groaned from his seat at the table in Candace's office. "I can't look at any more budget numbers today. My eyes are seeing double."

Candace glanced at the clock. "Go. It's late. This will be here tomorrow."

Just as she said that, a nearby explosion rocked the palace, shaking the walls. Asher grabbed Miriam and pushed her to the floor, covering her with his body. Miriam's heart pounded, and she grabbed at Asher's shoulders.

"Are you okay?" Asher asked.

Miriam was too shocked to speak. Asher sat up and looked around for Candace. The queen huddled under her desk. She crawled out and stood, dusting off her dress. "What the fuck?" She pressed the panic button on her desk. Moments later, Leah rushed into the room.

"Your Majesty! Are you all right?"

"I am. Are you?"

"Yes," Leah said. "The explosion was outside the perimeter, but it was big enough to shake us up. We've got the robotic force scanning for more explosives."

"How did they get close enough?" Miriam asked. She pulled herself into a standing position, taking Asher's offered hand.

"I don't know," Leah admitted. "I think we need to expand the perimeter. We need more robots and people. There's just no substitute for a soldier's instincts."

"Do what you need to do." Candace waved a hand. "Go. They need you."

Miriam trembled. She'd spent so much of her life in fear, but nothing like this. Asher grabbed her hand, his palms clammy. She took deep breaths, trying to calm her nerves. He squeezed her hand, and she relaxed into his touch. They were okay.

For now.

Candace rubbed her eyes. "Go down to the Residence. Explain what happened and check on everyone." She ran a hand through her hair. "Fuck. This is bad."

"Call Alderman," Miriam advised, her voice shaky. "He needs to know."

The queen nodded. "I'll be downstairs to check on everyone in a little while."

Asher placed his hand on the small of Miriam's back as they made their way to the elevator. Once inside, Miriam collapsed into his arms. He kissed the top of her head. "We're safe, Miriam."

"For how long?" A sob caught in her throat.

Asher didn't respond. The palace was supposed to be safe. What if the next attack made it past the perimeter? Miriam supposed all they could do was trust that increasing security would work.

"It had to be one of the justices," she said, thinking out loud. "I don't think a group of citizens could have made it that close and caused such a big explosion."

The elevator dinged as they reached the first floor. Asher sighed. "You're probably right. I wonder if we'll ever know for sure."

"Candace has spies in every mercenary force. Hopefully, we can get some answers." They stopped outside the Residence door, ignoring the robot that now guarded the entrance. "Hey. Thanks for, you know, saving me."

Asher's lip lifted in the corner. "You mean jumping on top of you? I didn't hurt you, did I?"

"No."

"I didn't even think, Miriam. I just needed you to be safe." He froze, his brow furrowed as if he wanted to say more, but he didn't.

Miriam smiled sadly. "Thank you."

The blocky robot scanned their bodies with a beep, then stepped aside to reveal the retina scanner. The door slid open, revealing the harem residents all in the main room. Miriam stepped inside. Sherah sobbed as Esther held her close. Daniel was pacing, nearly wearing a hole in the ornate rugs. Abel sat frozen, his eyes wide in shock, with a teary-eyed Marah sitting next to him.

Elijah leapt up when he saw Miriam and Asher. "What the hell happened?"

"There was an attack just outside the perimeter," Asher said. "We're safe. They're increasing security and looking for any more explosives."

Sherah let out a wail. Isaac wiped his eyes. His hands shook so fiercely, Miriam could see it from across the room.

"Candace said she'll be down in a little while. She should have more news for us then." Miriam went to sit next to Sherah. "Shh. We're okay now."

Daniel stopped pacing and turned to face Miriam. "Are we, though?"

Miriam had no answer. There were too many questions, too many unknowns. It was easier when the threats were far away, just footage on a screen. But now the reality had set in. They were in the midst of a civil war, and they were the lovers of the queen so many people wanted to overthrow. She couldn't shake the feeling that they were sitting ducks and that she needed to *do* something. She'd always been a person of action, with her Lady Lilith persona. Now, when it mattered most, all she could do was wait.

Half an hour later, Candace knocked on the door of the harem. Asher let her in, and everyone turned to face her.

"First, I want to assure you all that we're safe. We didn't find anything else. We've increased the perimeter and added more security. No one can get within a full mile of the palace." She inhaled before continuing. "However, after speaking with Alderman and our other allies from the Supreme Court, it's clear that we will be spread thin as the war ramps up. Gideon Thomas is increasing production of military robots and drones, as well as nanotech for field hospitals."

Her shoulders slumped. "I've been avoiding this because I don't even know where to start. But we need help."

"What do you mean?" Miriam asked.

"I mean, we need help from outside the country. I don't have friends in other places. No one will give me an audience."

Everyone waited for her to continue. The tension in the air was thick. Miriam leaned forward.

"I need to send someone to Mexico," Candace said. She blew out a breath. "But I don't trust just anyone. I want to send one or two of you."

"How will they get there?" Elijah asked.

"There are openings in the border wall along the DMZ. I can send someone in a car, along with a letter from me. If you can make it to the refugee camps along the Rio Grande, you'll need to find someone with some authority and explain what's going on." She shook her head. "I don't even know if it will work, but it's our best chance."

Asher's eyes met Miriam's. He raised an eyebrow, and Miriam gave him a small smile in agreement. This was her chance to do something more than sit around waiting. "I'll go."

"Me, too," Asher said.

Candace's shoulders slumped. "You two make the most sense. You know the most. But I don't know what I'll do without you."

"You've got a harem full of brilliant minds, Candace." Miriam patted Sherah on the knee. "Let them in."

"This is our war, too," Elijah said.

Candace nodded. "You're right." She clapped her hands together. "Okay, give me two days to make arrangements. Pack your bags, Asher and Miriam. You're going on a mission."

34

Asher stared at the freshly generated suitcase that lay empty on his bed. He'd spent the better part of a decade here in the harem, and now he was leaving in two days. He pulled at his shirt collar, nervous. Fifty miles of desert stretched between him and another country. What would it be like? He'd heard idyllic rumors about the clean air and the plentiful resources. Everyone was equal. There was no wicked Supreme Court, no monarchy. He wondered how much was true and how much was a tall-tale desperate Americans told as they dreamed of a better world.

Miriam was quick to volunteer, and against his better judgment, Asher had stepped up, too. He wasn't cut out for top-secret missions in foreign countries. But Miriam's bravery inspired him. And if he was honest with himself, he couldn't bear to be without her.

He threw down the bundle of clothes in his arms. He had to talk to her before they were all alone and far from home. If there was a chance she would forgive him, he had to take it, and he had to do it now.

Resolved, he crossed the hallway to Miriam's room and knocked on the door. "Come in!"

The door slid open at her command, and he stepped inside. "Hey. Can we talk?"

Miriam set down a pile of folded clothes in her own suitcase, then turned to him with a smile. "Sure. Are you also unsure what to pack for a political trip to Mexico?"

He chuckled. "I don't remember how to pack anything."

"Yeah," she said. "You've been here a long time." She pushed her dark hair out of her face. "What's up?

He chewed his lip as he gathered his thoughts. Miriam's gaze dropped to his mouth briefly before meeting his eyes again. His mouth was dry when he spoke. "Miriam, I fucked up, and I'm sorry."

Miriam heaved a sigh and sat down on her bed. "It's okay."

He scraped his hand through his hair. "No. It's not. I blamed you for something that wasn't your fault at all. That wasn't fair to you."

"Oh, Asher." She tilted her head with a small smile. Asher felt restless, twitchy, as he waited for her to respond. God, he needed her forgiveness like he needed water. "It wasn't fair. You're right. But I get it."

"How? I don't even get it, Miriam."

"You were ashamed. Angry. I was an easy target." She patted the bed next to her, and Asher sat down. He picked at his nails, unable to make eye contact with her. "You were hurting."

"But I hurt you, too."

"Yes. You did."

Her frankness pierced his heart. Miriam didn't mince words, but her tone was soft. Maybe it was pity, but he didn't want that. He studied her profile, the soft curve of her round cheeks, the fullness of her lips, and he realized then that he didn't just want her forgiveness. He wanted *her*. But he'd hurt her, and he didn't know how she'd ever take him back.

A stroke of bravery hit him like a lightning bolt. He had to try. He placed a tentative hand on her knee, and she shivered at his touch.

"Asher," she breathed. She looked down at his hand and frowned. "I don't know."

"Tell me what to do, Miriam. Tell me how to fix us."

They were silent for several long minutes, but Asher made no attempt to move his hand. Eventually, she settled hers on top of his and stroked her thumb across his sensitive skin. Finally, she broke the tension and cleared her throat. "You've got to stop hiding behind your grief and self-loathing."

Asher's voice cracked. "Lately, the only thing I've grieved is you."

Miriam's eyes welled with tears. Her throat bobbed as she swallowed. Asher had the urge to lean down and lick her neck, but now wasn't the time. "You're always going to grieve Bethany, Asher. But you can't let yourself live in a prison of shame anymore. You have to let me in. You have to be yourself again."

"I don't want to live in this prison anymore, Miriam. But I don't know how to let you—or anyone—in."

"Yes, you do. You had already started. Talk about her. Talk about what happened and what you're feeling." She leaned her head against his shoulder, overwhelming Asher with how right it felt. "And don't push me away when you're hurting."

She was right. Asher couldn't have her until he opened himself up, but the prospect was terrifying. He'd spent so long avoiding any feelings except shame and guilt that he wasn't sure how to feel anything else. But Miriam had given him a glimpse of healing and happiness. In a couple of days, they'd be free of this place that held so many painful memories. Briefly, the thought to abandon Candace and live a new, happy life with Miriam in Mexico crossed his mind. He couldn't do that to his best friend and queen, of course. Not when so many lives were at stake. It was a nice dream, though.

"I don't want to push you away again, Miriam. I can't live without you."

She folded her hand into his and squeezed. "You can, though, Asher. You're strong enough."

His heart sank. She didn't want him. He blinked against the burning wetness in his eyes.

"I don't want you to live without me, though."

He raised his head. "Really?"

"Asher, you're the first person I've ever fallen in love with. And I think you might be the last."

His lips crashed onto hers then, and she gasped into his mouth. He loved her more than he'd ever loved anyone, and he needed to show her. To let her feel his love from the depths of his soul. Her mouth opened, and he darted his tongue inside. Her kiss was salvation, and he drank it up like it was the finest vintage wine. She shifted, wrapping her arms around his neck and pulling him closer. He pulled her onto his lap so he could deepen the kiss and feel her body flush against his.

His hands grabbed her ample hips hard enough that it would leave a mark. Blood rushed to his cock, and she ground against his growing erection. God, how he'd missed her touch, her taste, her smell. They kissed for what could have been days, for all the sense of time Asher had. Finally, Miriam pulled away, gasping for air.

"Asher, we have to finish packing, and we have a meeting with

Candace soon."

"Fuck." He groaned.

She placed a peck on his lips. "We can finish this later."

"Promise?"

She nodded. "I promise. I love you, Asher. There's no one else I'd rather flee through the DMZ with."

He grinned then, and a warmth flooded through his core. "I love you, Miriam."

35

They were too busy and too tired to continue their reconciliation that night. Asher fell asleep with his arms wrapped around Miriam, dreaming of thirst in a never-ending desert. The next day was full of training by intelligence, meetings with Candace, and a goodbye party from the harem residents. Miriam had slipped away during the party, and Asher finally pulled himself from the conversation and went to check on her.

He found her curled in her bed with tears streaming down her face. "Miriam? What's wrong?"

She sat up. Her face was blotchy and wet. "Asher, I'm scared."

Understandably. The plane to the border wall left in twelve hours. A car would be waiting for them near an opening used by refugees fleeing the Holy USA. Then they would be alone, with no way to contact Candace until they found internet again. If they found it. Would they be turned away because of their association with the queen? The country had been locked down tight from outside contact for so many years. While the rest of the world progressed, American had devolved.

He sat down next to her and wrapped his arm around her shoulder. "We've got each other."

She wiped at her eyes. Without warning, she pushed him back

on the bed and straddled him. Her mouth nipped at his lips. "Fuck me, Asher."

He pushed her into a sitting position and studied her face. "Are you sure now's the right time?"

"I need to forget. I need to not feel anything for a little while."

"Miriam…"

"I'm putting myself at your mercy, Asher. Do whatever you want to me."

He recalled their conversation weeks ago. Miriam, always wound so tightly in control, craved release, but she'd never given herself over to anyone. Now she was asking Asher, giving herself over to him. He didn't deserve this level of trust, not so soon after they'd made amends. Yet she tugged on something dark and hot inside of him. He wanted her at his mercy, ached to see her finally let go.

He flipped her over onto her back and stood. "Be right back."

"Where are you going?" She propped herself up on her elbows. "I need you."

He smirked. "I know you do," he said in a husky voice. "Trust me. I'll be back in a second."

In his room, he gathered supplies he'd taken from Candace's wardrobe. When he returned, Miriam was in the same position. Her eyes twinkled as he held out a large, wand-style vibrator and a belt.

"Where'd you get that?"

"Borrowed it." He'd wanted to make their first sex since the breakup spectacular. The belt was an impulse move. He figured she'd balk at it, but so far, she just looked intrigued. His voice dropped as he said, "Take off your clothes."

Miriam closed her eyes and inhaled, and he expected her to

fight back against his command. Instead, she lifted her black t-shirt over her head, revealing her large breasts. He loved that she never wore a bra. Her nipples were tight buds, and he wanted to take them in his mouth. Not yet, he told himself.

She shimmied her shorts and panties off and cast them aside. Then she spread her legs, revealing her already glistening pussy. "How do you want me?"

What he wanted was to slam his cock into her post-haste. But that's not what this was about. It's not what she needed. He swallowed hard. "Put your hands above your head."

She obeyed, and he climbed over her to secure her wrists in his generated-leather belt. She squirmed, and he swatted her leg. "Stay still."

"Yes, sir."

Asher's eyes widened. No one had called him sir since...he pushed the memory out of his mind. Instead, he let her words awaken something that was sleeping deep within him.

"Good girl," he breathed in her ear.

She whimpered, and the sound shot straight to his cock. He kissed her, plundering her mouth and biting her lips. Her streak of submissiveness didn't dampen the fire within her, and she met him stroke for stroke. She struggled against the belt, and he placed a hand on her wrists as his lips worked their way down her neck to her breasts. He placed gentle kisses along the tops before capturing one hard nipple in his mouth. He sucked hard, and she writhed beneath him.

Using his free hand, he pinched the other nipple as his teeth teased the first one. Then he switched. Miriam's flesh was scorching beneath him, and he hadn't even brought out his new toy.

He released her wrists and slid his hand over her curvy stomach to the thatch of dark hair between her thighs. He kept his hand there, and she arched her hips to try to lower his touch.

"Naughty, naughty." He bit at her earlobe.

"Aren't you going to take your clothes off?" she asked, her voice low and sultry.

He buried his face between her breasts and shook his head. "Not yet," he said, muffled by her full tits.

After torturing her long enough, he gently placed a finger on her clit. She gasped.

"More."

"More what?"

"More, please." Her eyes fluttered closed. "Sir."

He forced her knees apart and stroked her soaking core. He started slowly, even as her hips beckoned him to increase the speed and pressure. But he wasn't ready for her to come yet. Moving his fingers lower, he stuck two inside her. She bucked and groaned.

He pumped his fingers until he felt her walls begin to tighten, then he removed them. She swore in disappointment, and he laughed. He reached for the vibrator.

"Your job," he told her, "is to come until you can't come anymore."

A wide smile lit up her face. "Orgasm torture. How did you know?"

"I know what you need, baby. Look at me." She opened her eyes. "Red, yellow, green. Got it?"

"Red, yellow, green," she repeated. A flush of doubt washed over Asher, and somehow, she knew. "I trust you, Asher."

That was enough for him. He flipped the switch on the

vibrator, and it whirred to life. Miriam's eyes widened, and her knees fell further apart. Slowly, he lowered the pulsating head to her clit.

36

Miriam cried out as the wand touched her throbbing clit. She threw her head back. Somehow, she wanted to pull away and get more simultaneously. She fought against the urge to close her legs, taking a deep breath to steady her trembling.

That thing was merciless. Within less than a minute, Miriam came with a shout. She could feel the wet spot on the bed growing beneath her. How had she lived her whole life without a device like this?

Asher pulled the toy away, and she immediately felt its loss. Still, the aftershocks of her first orgasm quaked through her. He gave her only a couple minutes of reprieve before settling the wand against her again. She let out a long moan that was half-pain, half-pleasure. Asher stared at her with heat in his eyes. "You all right?"

"Green." She gasped as he pressed a button to increase the vibrations. "Holy fuck!"

"You are such a good little slut." He ran his free hand over her breasts and tweaked a nipple. Miriam arched her back off the bed, which forced more pressure from the vibrator onto her clit.

Another orgasm crashed over her. He lowered his mouth to her breasts as she rode out the wave of ecstasy, but he did not remove the device from between her legs. It stayed in place as her body shook. It ached, and yet, she didn't want it to end. She spread her legs even wider, earning a sultry chuckle from Asher. Sadist that he was, he pulled away and flipped off the vibrator.

"No," she moaned. Her heart was a jackhammer, her breathing rapid. "Don't stop."

"Oh, I have no plans to." He sunk to his knees and jerked her to the edge of the bed. He placed tender kisses along the insides of her thighs, his warm breath inching closer to her wanton pussy. Finally, finally, he swirled his tongue around her swollen clit. He made a sound of delight.

Miriam's clit was beyond sensitive by this point. Yet, she ground against his face as he licked and sucked. His pace was slower than the wand, but no less pleasurable. Her tender nerve-endings were on fire, and within a few minutes, she coasted through yet another orgasm.

This time, he gave her no rest. Instead, he plunged two fingers inside of her, curling them toward her G-spot. Her hips raised off the bed, and he pushed them down with his other hand. Miriam strained against the belt that tied her hands, whimpering as he relentlessly forced her toward yet another orgasm.

"More, damn it!"

"You're bossy."

She raised her head and glared at him. "I am who I am."

"And I love you for it. Lie back."

She didn't fight him. She closed her eyes to lose herself to the sensations of his strong, thrumming fingers inside of her. He brushed his thumb over her clit as he slid a third finger inside her core. She was dripping, and the noises coming from his pumping hand aroused her even further. The vibrator buzzed to life, and a wave of anticipatory fear washed over her. "I don't know if I can."

"Are you safe-ing out?"

"Fuck no. Green green green."

The head of the wand grazed her clit, and she screamed. If anyone could hear her—and she was sure they could—they'd be quite concerned. She pulsed her pussy against the toy. It hurt, and she couldn't stop. Her body was weakening, and she didn't think she could come again, but she chased the orgasm anyway. She was close. So close. She just needed a little more.

Asher intuitively knew it, too. He withdrew his hand from her soaking pussy and teased one finger over her rear entrance. It was exactly what she needed, and she came, shouting Asher's name.

"That's it, baby."

Tears streamed down Miriam's cheeks. Her skin crackled with tension. She was utterly spent. The stack of orgasms had wrung her dry. Or so she thought.

She heard a zipper. "I can't wait any longer, Miriam. I need to be inside of you."

He plunged his hard cock deep within her, sheathing himself in one stroke. Her swollen flesh made her feel even fuller than normal. She wept openly now, and Asher leaned down to kiss away her tears. "You're doing so good, baby."

"I can't...I can't..."

"You can." He pumped his hips in a slow and steady motion. Capturing her mouth with his, he stroked against her tongue as his erection stroked her inner walls. Miriam wrapped her legs around him and pulled him deeper. He sped up his ministrations, and Miriam felt pressure building all over again.

"Harder," she moaned, urging him ever deeper.

He snapped his hips fast and hard. Miriam rocked against him, delighting in the pressure against her clit. She clenched around him as her orgasm crept up, and they came together. He groaned against her lips as he drained himself inside her.

He withdrew and collapsed next to her on the bed. Miriam was shaking, and even the brush of his arm against hers was too much. Her limbs were feather light, and she swore she was sinking straight into the bed. Every time she closed her eyes, she saw stars, as if she were rushing through time and space. Asher kissed her bare shoulder, sending shivers all over her body.

"How do you feel?" he asked in a low voice.

"Mm," was all she could manage to say.

He laughed. "Good." He stood and zipped up his pants.

"Where are you going?" It came out as a pathetic whine.

"To get you some water. I'll be right back, I promise."

It could have been seconds or hours before he returned. Miriam was floating in bliss, unaware of time. Eventually, he slipped back into the room; Miriam was vaguely aware of her door opening. He nudged her.

"Sit up. Drink some water."

She wanted to argue, but she couldn't find the energy. She grunted as she pulled herself into a sitting position. "I feel like I'm going to float away."

"Good." He lifted the cup of water to her lips. The cool liquid washed down her throat, grounding her more in the present. "What do you need? Do you want a shower?"

She laid back down and shook her head against the pillow. "Just hold me. But take off your clothes first."

"Ready for a round two already?" He lifted his shirt above his head, revealing his toned chest and a smattering of brown hair.

"Hardly. I just want to feel close to you."

He stepped out of his pants and slipped into the bed next to Miriam. Wrapping his arms around her, he whispered, "You have me."

And she did. She trusted him with her body, her vulnerability. He was learning to trust her—and himself.

Tomorrow would bring the unknown. They'd traverse the desert, with only each other for support and company. They had no idea if they could find help in Mexico, but they had to try. Could they even contact Candace once they made it through the DMZ? So much uncertainty. Yet, for the first time, one thing was certain. They had each other, and whatever happened next, that was enough.

Epilogue

The desert stretched around them, shades of beige and brown and deep, dusky red. A few minutes ago, they'd passed through a hole in the border fence just big enough for a car. Miriam drove. The road was old and worn, and every few seconds, they bumped over a hole.

Candace had seen them off from her private jet. It was risky for her to be away from the safety of the palace, but she had insisted. She gave them a Moses Tablet and a solar charging pad. "Contact me as soon as possible," she had said. "And take care of yourselves."

If someone had told Miriam four months ago that she'd cry saying goodbye to the queen, she'd have laughed in their face. But she had. Even Asher teared up as he hugged his friend farewell.

Now they were alone. Neither had spoken as they sped off on the ancient highway toward Ciudad Juárez, Mexico. Candace's intelligence had said there was a refugee camp along the Rio Grande, fifty miles from the border fence.

"Hey, what's that?" Asher asked, breaking the heavy silence. They were only about ten miles into their journey.

Miriam slowed down and squinted. "It says water." She glanced over at Asher. "Want to stop?"

He shrugged. "Just pull over."

They pulled alongside the sign to find several cases of water in glass bottles. "That's odd."

"Yeah. I wonder who put that there." He sighed. "I guess we should keep going."

Miriam sped off again, swerving to avoid the largest potholes. And she thought roads inside the Holy USA were bad. Five miles later, they spotted another sign. This time, they got out, and each grabbed a granola bar from a large trunk. The desert sun beat down on them. Sweat beaded down Miriam's temples in seconds. Thank goodness the old car Candace had loaned them had air conditioning.

The next sign was massive, rising out of the desert landscape like a sunrise. In big, bold letters, it read, "Freedom Awaits. Keep Going."

Asher and Miriam looked at each other, eyes wide. "How many people do you think are fleeing?"

He shrugged. "It seems like more than we had guessed."

But it was at the thirty-mile mark that the shock truly set in. "What the fuck?" Miriam whispered. She slowed the car as they drove past several buildings. A massive greenhouse glinted in the sunshine. Several small but sturdy huts wrapped around the greenhouse in a half-circle. Just beyond the buildings was a small water tower. Solar panels dotted the sand all around.

There were people. People! A few stopped and stared at the car. Some waved, while others just smiled. Children ran around, laughing and playing. Miriam even spotted a dog near one of the huts.

"I thought this was a no-man's-land," Asher said. He raised a hand to wave at the people.

"Surely Candace would have told us if she knew."

"Yeah. I don't think she has any clue. Let's keep going."

A few miles down, the highway smoothed into fresh pavement. Another small village, almost identical to the last, appeared out of nowhere. Just like at the first one, people waved and smiled as they drove past. Miriam was curious and wanted to stop, but they had a mission. They passed more water stops and one more village before the fifty-mile mark crept up on them. They drove through rubble and abandoned buildings that once comprised El Paso.

"Holy shit," Asher breathed. His hand grabbed Miriam's knee. "Look."

The Rio Grande snaked along the banks before them. The highway ended at a large bridge. Miriam had expected a tent city full of malnourished children and weary adults when Candace talked about refugee camps. Instead, small houses, similar to those they'd passed in the DMZ, dotted the landscape beyond the river, along with some larger buildings. The sun reflected off of rooftop solar panels.

A large sign hung from the bridge that read, "Welcome, Americans."

Miriam inched closer, expecting to see armed guards or robots. Instead, there were two people wearing bright orange vests and holding tablets. They waved the car forward. Miriam and Asher rolled down their windows and came to a stop in the middle of the bridge.

One of the workers came up to Asher's window. "Welcome! We just need to get your information, then we can find you a place to stay. Can I scan your chips, or would you prefer to give me your information manually?"

Miriam and Asher looked at each other. "We don't have chips."

"Oh!" The person looked shocked. "Well, that's okay. We don't use them here, anyway. It just makes getting your information easier." They furrowed their brow. "What brings you to Mexico?"

They said the country's name in Spanish, even though they spoke perfect English.

Asher heaved a deep breath. "We're here on behalf of Her Majesty the Queen."

The worker waved over their partner, who came to Miriam's window and leaned down, confusion on their face. "¿Que paso?"

"The Supreme Court has turned on the throne. We're in the midst of a civil war," Asher continued, his voice careful. Steady. "We come seeking aid."

Miriam's heart was in her throat as she waited for their response. Candace had no allies in this hemisphere and only a few on the other side of the world. Would they be turned away? Arrested?

"Well, we thought this day would never come," the first worker said with a genuine smile. "Let's get you to the embassy."

Asher reached for Miriam's hand. Their eyes met. This was it. Whatever came next, they faced together.

Coming Soon

T he *American Harem* series continues in *American Trinity* with Jonathan, Elijah, and Esther's love story. Scan here to pre-order:

Coming Soon

The *American Harem* series continues in *American Trinity* with Jonathan, Elijah, and Esther's love story. Scan here to pre-order:

About the Author

Krystal N. Craiker is an indie romance author, freelance writer, and editor. She has a background in anthropology and education, which brings fresh perspectives to her romance novels. When she's not daydreaming about her next book or article, you can find her cooking gourmet gluten-free cuisine, laughing at memes, and playing board games. Krystal lives in Dallas, Texas with her husband, child, and dog. Follow her on Instagram(@krystalncraikerauthor).